BEST FRIENDS, BIKINIS, AND OTHER SUMMER CATASTROPHES

BEST FRIENDS, BIKINIS,
AND OTHER
SUMMER
CATASTROPHES

Kristi Wientge

Simon & Schuster Books for Young Readers

NEW YORK LONDON TORONTO SYDNEY NEW DELHI

SIMON & SCHUSTER BOOKS FOR YOUNG READERS
An imprint of Simon & Schuster Children's Publishing Division
1230 Avenue of the Americas, New York, New York 10020

SIMON & SCHUSTER BOOKS FOR YOUNG READERS
and related marks are trademarks of Simon & Schuster, Inc.
For information about special discounts for bulk purchases, please contact
Simon & Schuster Special Sales at 1-866-506-1949 or business@simonandschuster.com.
The Simon & Schuster Speakers Bureau can bring authors to your live event.
For more information or to book an event, contact the Simon & Schuster Speakers Bureau
at 1-866-248-3049 or visit our website at www.simonspeakers.com.
Interior design by Hilary Zarycky
The text for this book was set in Berling.
Manufactured in the United States of America
0422 FFG
First Edition
2 4 6 8 10 9 7 5 3 1
CIP data for this book is available from the Library of Congress.
ISBN 9781534485020
ISBN 9781534485044 (ebook)

Grandma Sylvia (1939–1995)
Grandpa King (1937–2020)

CHAPTER ONE

School has been out for exactly thirty-two days. Will and I have already watched a horror movie in my basement (we kept the lights on, but next time we won't chicken out—or I'll at least bring down my little brothers' night-light) and finished off the extra-large pizza at Goodfellows (which barely fits between us in the back seat of the car without jabbing into our ribs), and today at the pool, the water is finally warm enough that our lips aren't turning blue. There's no new challenge for us here. The scariest thing is the high dive, and we've been jumping off that since we passed our swim test in second grade. We agreed that the pool would be a good place to come up with our next summer challenge, but so far Will is letting me make up the rules of the game and asking pointless questions like if he should get sunglasses or if his swimming shirt looks dumb.

"Look around, Alex. None of the other boys are wearing one," Will says, and pulls on the shirt. He's sitting across from me on a blow-up pool raft. The top of the raft is clear and you can see through it to the silvery bottom. It shimmers, and I half expect an answer to pop up like how it does in a Magic 8 Ball.

"Who cares?" I say. Since when does Will worry about what he looks like? My foot presses against the hot concrete, and I push us out into the middle of the water for our second round of Deep-Sea Diver. The diving sticks are in a pile between Will and me on the raft. My older brother, Brian, bought the raft for us with his employee discount at Big Lots. Even though he has a job, he's a cheapskate and wouldn't spend more than $3.99 on something we'll use all summer.

The sun hits the raft at a slight angle, reflecting right into my eyes.

I swear I only squint for a second.

One second feels like a forgettable moment, but things that happen in a single second might just change your whole summer.

One second. That's all it takes for Will to look away . . . and see Rebekah walk over.

Green bikini bottoms sit low on her hips, and the

top is a mix between a sports bra and a regular bra. She stops at the edge of the water, looks right at Will, and says, "Hi. Do you guys want to get ice cream?"

I know Rebekah is not asking me, even though she said "you guys." Her eyes are trained on Will.

Will practically jumps off the raft.

"What about the dolphins?" I yell. I want to say something that only Will understands, but once I hear it out loud, I feel like a little kid. It was my idea to pretend the diving sticks are dolphins.

He doesn't even turn around as he follows her to the snack bar.

Rebekah does. She gives me this confused smile like she's trying to be nice. But do nice people steal your best friend when you're in the middle of a game? I'll answer that for you. No.

As she turns back to Will and they make their way to the other side of the community pool, I can't hear her, but she moves her mouth to say what looks like "dolphin." Her hands turn up to the sky like she put a question mark after it. I dip my face underwater to cool my cheeks down. I should have just said "diving sticks."

I squint hard at Will's back. The back I've seen slathered in mud when we played war in the creek; that was covered in poison ivy the time we unknowingly lay in a bed of it, eating mulberries from Mrs. Branson's trees. It's a back with the right shoulder blade sticking out more than the left because of his scoliosis. I wait for Will to explain to Rebekah that Deep-Sea Diver is only the best game ever but she can't play because it's our game.

Instead he shrugs, and orders his usual chocolate éclair ice cream from his mom, who runs the snack bar. Rebekah orders a plain vanilla cone. Figures. Even though Rebekah has gone to school with us since we were eight, Will and I don't know too much about her. She's always hung out with the more popular kids. But you can tell a lot about a person's character from their ice cream selection.

She leads him to a table in the shade. Will slides onto the bench. Rebekah waits and slides right next to him. Will scoots over a little more, but Rebekah just laughs and scoots so close that their arms touch!

The only reason Rebekah probably even said hello was for free dessert.

Rebekah says something that makes Will laugh. His real laugh is loud and comes out in *ba-ha*s instead of *ha-ha*s, which makes me laugh harder. But his laugh right now is way too shrill for a twelve-year-old boy. It sounds more like a yelp. Their mouths move and they keep smiling and eating. Which, by the way, looks disgusting.

I turn away and paddle out to the middle of the deep end. Paddling with one arm while holding diving sticks in the other makes me spin in circles. I yank on my one-piece as it rides up with all the paddling. You can't deep-sea dive in a bikini.

I imagine myself in the middle of the ocean. I take a deep breath, filling my mouth with the sour, salty ocean smell, letting it burn all the way up through my nose and deep into my chest. The squeals of the little kids in the baby pool are seagulls. Unlike Will, I have a great imagination. I create all the games we play, and if I were going to ditch him for someone else, I'd choose someone way more imaginative than plain-vanilla-cone Rebekah Benton.

Still, when I close my eyes, all I can see is Will talking to Rebekah. What could he possibly be saying to her? Didn't she notice the way the chocolate cookie pieces stuck to his bottom lip when he laughed? Or was that why she was laughing? Like chocolate crumbs and melted vanilla ice cream are *so* funny.

Whatever. I have more important stuff to do anyway. I lob the diving sticks into the water one by one.

After counting to ten slowly, I roll off the back of the raft like scuba divers do and sink to the bottom of the pool. It's important to collect as many diving sticks as I can before coming up for air. There are only three left, but my lungs are about to burst. Who knew your best friend talking to a girl in a bikini could be so distracting?

I hang onto the side of the raft for a few extra moments and arrange the sticks. I don't care if Will and Rebekah are practically sitting on top of each other at the snack bar eating ice cream. Everyone knows the ice cream is way better at Mr. Dreamy's on Main Street.

I head back underwater, grab the three diving sticks, and pretend to struggle with a fishing net, but manage to break away at the last minute.

"Alex!"

Will stands at the side of the pool, smiling at me as I surface. I smile back and wipe hair out of my face. I knew Rebekah only wanted free ice cream.

"Hey, can I borrow the raft? Rebekah and I want to float on it."

Rebekah walks up beside Will. "Hey."

Did she forget she already said hello to me?

I open my mouth. The only reason I can think to

say no is because I don't want Rebekah on our raft, which isn't the best reason. Technically Brian gave the raft to both Will and me, and Will had used just as much of his breath blowing this raft up as I had.

Since I don't say anything, Will takes my silence as a yes and reaches in to pull the raft toward him. The diving sticks fall into the water. Will doesn't even notice. Instead he waves his arm in this dramatic way that makes Rebekah laugh.

Really loud.

She holds on to the edge of the pool as she slides her legs across the surface and lies back, barely getting a splash on her. Who comes to a pool and tries to stay dry?

Will dives over her, even though you're not allowed to dive anywhere but the diving board area. I swear, if Rebekah laughs again, that float is going over.

She doesn't, but I also don't see my raft for the rest of the afternoon.

CHAPTER TWO

The thing about Will is, he's practically my fourth brother. We've grown up right next door to each other since kindergarten. Sometimes we act more like brother and sister. Which, if you ask me, is better than being best friends.

So at first I pretend Will didn't completely ditch me. Even though his questions about swim shirts and sunglasses echo around in my head, making my stomach feel like I swallowed a gallon of pool water.

Janice and Tanya are at the diving boards. I'm not best friends with them or anything. We run cross-country together, so we're more like friends who hang out on the bus after meets and occasionally at school. I figure it's better to join them than sit by myself at the side of the pool—especially now that I don't have a raft to distract me. "Hey, are you guys having a diving contest?" I ask.

"No," Janice says. Her hand goes to her hip. She's wearing a one-piece with stripes down the side; sometimes meanness isn't as obvious as Rebekah's bright green two-piece bathing suit.

For a minute I think Janice is going to laugh or tell me to get lost. Then a smile spreads wide across her face, erasing my worries. "But that'd be awesome."

"I'll judge," Tanya says.

It just so happens that the guard on duty for the diving pool is Samantha, my older brother's girlfriend. "We'll ask the lifeguard to judge," I tell them, and turn my head to the stand. "Hey, Samantha," I call, even though it'd be easier to call her Sam, the same way I go by Alex instead of Alexandria.

The first time Brian brought her home, she insisted on being called Sa-man-tha. She even said it like each syllable had its own zip code.

"Can you judge our dives?" I ask.

Samantha swings a whistle around her fingers a few times and shrugs. "Whatever."

The three of us climb up our ladders. It takes Janice the longest because she's on the high dive. Tanya and I are on the lower boards.

"One. Two. Three," Samantha calls.

I dive, pointing my toes just right and keeping my arms pin-straight as I hit the water.

"You in the blue," Samantha says, pointing to Tanya. "You win."

"You can't judge it like that," I say. Samantha has no imagination. Which makes me think of Will, but I've got a diving contest to win, so I remain focused. "You have to choose who's first, second, and third."

"Okay, then you, you, and you," Samantha says, pointing at each of us.

"All right, Tanya, you get three points. Janice, you get two, and I get one."

We switch boards and go again.

Samantha chooses Janice, me, and then Tanya this time. She isn't really paying attention to us, but we keep score anyway.

"This time let's see who makes the biggest splash," Janice says.

"Okay, Samantha?" I call.

"Yeah, sure. It's almost time for my break."

I'm glad I have the high dive for this one because I need all the help I can get. It's not only my lack of boobs that keeps me from looking like Rebekah in a bikini. It's a lack of pretty much anything.

I run and hold my knees to my chest, waiting

for the crash of water around me. Underwater, tiny bubbles explode, tickling my skin as I sink to the bottom. This is what summer's all about. The only thing missing is Will. My thoughts keep going back to him on that raft with Rebekah. On *our* raft. On the first warm-water day of *our* summer.

The summer that I thought was going well now has me wondering if maybe Will wanted this summer to be different. Or if maybe horror movies, pizza, and pool games aren't enough.

I break through the surface, turning to Samantha, hoping the high dive gave me an advantage.

She's looking over at the snack bar, where the clock hangs. "Break time," she says, throwing her head back and sighing. Another lifeguard walks toward her chair. "See you later for s'mores, Alex." She climbs down the ladder.

"Who won?" I yell after her.

"You're all winners." She flashes a fake smile and keeps walking.

"We've gotta go anyway," Tanya says. "My mom's waving us over."

"Okay, see ya." I swim to the ladder and climb out. It's hard not to look for Will. I have to stop myself once I realize I'm doing it.

"Alex." Will pops up next to me. "My mom said we can have these for our walk home." He holds out two Fudgsicles.

The concrete is hot under my feet, and my eyes burn from my jumping in and out of the water, making me feel tired. I really want to enjoy this moment. The routine of summer—my eyes burning from the chlorine, my skin tingling from the sun, and the comfort of walking home with Will while we eat our Popsicles. I don't want to ruin it by being mad at him.

So I take the Fudgsicle that Will holds out to me and decide not to ask where Rebekah is.

On the walk home I wonder why Will getting ice cream with Rebekah even bothers me. She's been going to school with us since third grade. It's not like we hang out with any of the same people, but she's the kind of girl everyone notices even if you're not friends with her. And now she's noticed Will.

I look over at Will, who is completely focused on his Fudgsicle—which he eats with about as many manners as he did tackling that chocolate éclair ice cream in front of Rebekah earlier—none. I bet his mom had forgotten that he'd eaten ice cream about an hour ago when she offered him these.

This reminds me of the time when his dog died. He'd been sad for days. That weekend, we sat in our tree and he looked too serious, so I asked him what he was thinking about. His answer: "I'm craving a burger."

Mom says boys' needs are primal. She tried to get into a much deeper talk about boys and girls when I asked her how my brothers and dad could eat two whole pizzas at the hospital a few hours after Nana died.

Will and I both have times during the year when we're busy with other people. Will because of swim team or me when it's cross-country season. But all the in-between moments, like after school, weekends, and summer—it's just the two of us. Rebekah was different from swim team. I can't quite explain how, but I never felt like swim team was stealing Will away.

Will was only with her about an hour, and already tiny worms of worry are wiggling in my stomach. I worked so hard trying to think of fun things for Will and me to do this summer, and all Rebekah had to do was ask if he wanted ice cream.

That might not sound like a big deal, but I have three brothers. Only Brian is old enough to notice girls, but that's taught me enough. When a boy jumps out of the water for someone, leaving the other person in the middle of a game, it's possible he'll follow that girl for weeks or months.

Since Will seems to have forgotten whatever happened today at the pool to focus on eating, I decide I can let it slide too. Besides, Will isn't like Brian. At all.

Will uses his teeth to eat the last piece of his Fudgsicle before throwing the stick into the grass.

"Will!" He knows I hate it when he does that.

"It's made from natural material," he says. "I'm helping the birds make sturdier nests."

I let out a low growl, pick it up, and hold it with mine. When I stand up, I notice our favorite house is right across the street.

This house has it all. A pool. A trampoline. A garden. Now someone is hammering a wooden structure up in the tree.

We both stop in the middle of the sidewalk.

"Tree house," we say at the same time, our minds sharing the exact same thought. And right in this moment, things are how they're supposed to be.

"Remember when we tried to build one?" Will says.

"Yeah. It would have been perfect." A couple of summers ago, Will and I begged our parents for our own supersecret hideaway. Too bad we kept hammering our fingers or nailing boards into the air instead of the tree. We didn't get very far before hanging out at the pool sounded a whole lot better.

We watch our neighbor bang away, the delayed echo of his hammering matching our footfalls.

Will turns down our block, but I look back one more time. My toes wiggle in my flip-flops as I think about what a tree house in the tree between our yards would look like. The frame of this one has little places cut out for windows. Scalloped edges swoop up and down along the roofline. It's like a dollhouse.

Our tree house would have windows up high enough for just Will and me to see out of, mostly to spy on our brothers. The roof wouldn't have fancy details. It wouldn't be a dollhouse; it would be a fort. An exclusive place just for us.

I run to catch up to Will. "I've got it. Our next summer challenge."

"Nothing beats my idea to get chickens and sell the eggs. Just a little more convincing, and I think my mom'll agree," Will says excitedly.

"But what if we don't have to do much convincing because we'll do all the work?"

Will stops. His cheeks are burned just at the tops,

right under his eyes. His hair is already a lighter brown from the sun. Same as every summer.

"We can finally build our tree house! My dad has all this wood in the garage left over from a million jobs. I bet we can get him to help if we promise to follow through and keep the yard picked up. He'd love it if you wanted to build something. Brian hates to even mow, much less use power tools."

Will nods as my idea settles into his thoughts. "It would be epic, wouldn't it?"

"Duh," I say. Our walking past the neighbors' tree house is a sign. Will needed to see how fun this summer could be. Like our muffin stand three summers ago and our hamster babysitting venture the following summer, and just last summer we had a pretty great Blow Pop business going at the pool until his mom realized we were taking them from the snack bar storage closet.

Maybe most of our ideas didn't exactly work out, but the tree house would be different. It would remind Will how much fun we have on our own. That *I'm* his best friend. That Rebekah is just a pesky distraction.

A tree house will hold everything in place.

CHAPTER THREE

Will and I sneak past my mom and two younger brothers, who are thankfully out on the back porch doing a craft. Before they can spot us, I wave Will over to the stairs. I was so happy when Mom and Dad surprised me with my new bedroom up in the attic just after my littlest brother, Josh, was born. It took me an entire year to convince Will it wasn't haunted. He'd read a book about a boy finding toys in his attic that came alive, and Will swore the stuffed animals in my room would attack him.

He pauses at the bottom of the stairs, but before he can come up with a lame excuse to avoid my room, I grab his arm and nudge him up in front of me.

"Look, if we want my dad's help with the tree house, we'll have to prove to him we're serious. And willing to fork over some cash."

"How are we going to do that?" Will looks around

my room, like he's waiting for an inanimate object to grab him.

"Will, I don't have any dolls, and Josh took all my stuffed toys. Nothing's going to get you." I push my watercolors aside and find my brush pens and inks. I grab my blotter pad and a fresh piece of paper and sit at my desk. "We're going to get a summer job."

"Job?" Will falls onto the beanbag chair under the window next to my desk.

"Yes, a job. And not our usual kind that doesn't make any money or gets us in trouble. How can we earn money fast?" I tap my chin with the handle of my blue brush pen. "What about mowing lawns?"

"We'd need a mower and gas and a way to get that stuff to other people's houses."

"We could weed flower beds," I say.

Will shrugs. "I'm not sure how much we'd get paid."

"Yeah, but it's one of those things everyone hates doing. People would rather give us some money instead of doing it themselves."

"I guess, but it really hurts my back." Will scrunches his nose and wiggles down deeper into the beanbag chair so I can hear the stuffing shift. "We should think bigger."

"Bigger?"

"Yeah. Let's just say we're willing to help out, do all the things people don't want to do. You know, wash the windows, clean the gutters, clean out sheds, and weed. Even though I hope people don't ask us to weed. All the stuff our parents complain about."

I nod along. "That's it."

I open the cap of my pen and write the first thing that comes into my head:

Messy yard?

Messy garage?

If you need help getting organized this summer,

Call:

Will and Alex's Services

555-0120

I put down Will's number since I don't have my own phone. It sounds snappy, like a commercial you'd hear on the radio.

The calligraphy for the text is clean and angled just right, but it looks empty, so I add some boxes overflowing with junk in the top left corner and a flower bed at the bottom. It's perfect.

"What do you think?" I ask, holding it up for Will to see.

"Services?" Will asks. "What if it's a cat lady? I can't bathe cats. I'm allergic."

I swallow down my sigh. "I promise, if it's a cat lady, I'll do the cat bathing."

"Then I'm in. When do we ask your dad?"

"After dinner. We're having s'mores. Come over and we'll talk to him then."

Will stands up. "Good idea. How could he say no if he's eating chocolate?" He collects his bag and I follow him downstairs.

"I'll make copies of this and we can pass them out tomorrow on the way to the pool."

"Okay. I'll see you later," Will calls, bumping into Brian as he and Samantha come through the side door.

"Whoa, what have you two lovebirds been up to?" Brian says in a childish voice. Samantha smiles next to him like she thinks Brian's joke is hilarious and the idea of Will and me having a crush on each other is cute at the same time. Luckily, Will is already gone.

"Shut up, Brian," I say, just as Mom walks in.

"Alexandria!" She says my name like I'm the one being a jerk, not Brian.

"But he said—"

Mom puts her hands up. "Nope. Not now. I have a

call that starts in exactly thirty seconds." She turns to Brian. "I need you to move the boxes Pops dropped off before someone trips and breaks something." She then looks at me. "I need you to get the hot dogs and s'mores ready. Dad will get the grill going when he gets home." She grabs her blazer off the back of a chair at the dining table. "Eat without me; I'll be out when it's s'mores time."

Brian waits until her office door clicks closed. "Yeah, so if you could move those boxes from Pops, I've got stuff to do."

He takes Samantha's hand and leads her outside.

Yeah, right. "Stuff."

I stomp toward the laundry room, where the boxes are. They're heavy and full of the yellow ice cream bowls we always used on the Fourth of July (part of Nana's fireworks-themed table setting) and the tall sundae glasses we'd use on New Year's Eve for Pops's famous ice cream bar. Ever since Nana died a year ago and Pops decided to sell the house, he's been leaving us boxes of things that he thinks we'll want to hang on to.

Or maybe he's just getting rid of what he doesn't want to remember.

The thing is, I want to remember. But Pops keeps

dropping the boxes off and we keep shoving them onto our shelves in the garage.

I put the box next to a stack of Nana's lilac-colored dessert plates, but take out a few of the yellow ice cream bowls and bring them inside with me. Then I pull the hot dogs out of the fridge and find the grilling tongs and platter that Dad uses. I'm collecting the buns, relish, mustard, and ketchup as Dad walks in. "Hey, kiddo. Let me wash up and I'll get the grill started."

Dad kicks off his work boots and scrubs his hands in the laundry room sink. "Your brothers outside?"

"Yeah. Mom said to start dinner without her."

"Aye, aye." He takes the platter and heads to the grill. I lean out the door and ask Brian, "Where are the graham crackers?"

Brian doesn't even look up from his phone. He just shoves his chin over toward the house.

It's like he doesn't realize talking was invented for a reason. It's way clearer than his chin-shoves and head-nods. "Oh, really. Inside?"

"Car."

"Wow. He can talk." I wait for him to go get the graham crackers from his car, but he doesn't move. He continues to tap his thumbs across his phone.

"Brian! Get. The. Graham. Crackers."

He puts his phone down. "I told you. They're in the car."

I look up at the ceiling. "So go get them," I say as nicely as possible.

Now Samantha drops her phone a few inches. They both stare at me.

"We can't have s'mores without the graham crackers." I let the door slam and grab Nana's bowls to fill with the s'mores ingredients. I open the chocolate and break it into pieces and fill the other one with marshmallows. I refuse to do all of Brian's work. If I have to move the boxes, he can walk to his car to get something for dessert.

Brian thinks he's so great because he drives and has a job where he actually gets paid money, but I still get stuck doing all the hard stuff. Like watching James, who's ten and thinks he doesn't need to listen to me, and Josh, who's six and does whatever James does. Plus, helping Mom with dinner whenever her calls go over. Without getting a single cent! Mom likes to say that it buys me privileges like staying up later than my younger brothers and watching movies at Will's on weekends.

I don't even like s'mores, and here I am. Setting it

all up. And what does Brian do? He probably grabbed the generic graham crackers from Big Lots that taste like dirt. He's too lazy to drive a mile to get the real graham crackers.

"Hot dogs are ready," Dad says, coming inside to place the tongs in the sink. "Let's get your brothers washed up to eat." He follows me out to the back porch.

"How's work?" he asks in Brian and Samantha's direction. They both shrug.

I usher James and Josh inside.

"Here, carry the ketchup," I tell James after he's sprinkled the air with warm water instead of wiping his hands with a dish towel.

He starts to push through the door like he didn't hear me, so I add, "Or else no s'mores."

He takes the ketchup off the counter, and Josh follows him out.

I grab the rest of the things we need for dinner and join everyone on the porch. James and Josh inhale their hot dogs and run off to play. Brian and Samantha eat and don't really talk, except to whisper and quietly laugh to each other. Mid-laugh, Brian reaches for the mustard, and Samantha makes a face. It's so small, I'm probably the only one who's paying enough attention to them to notice. But I watch Brian's hand move past it and grab the ketchup instead.

I roll my eyes and squirt extra mustard onto my hot dog, hoping she notices. Pops joked with me once that people who don't like mustard aren't to be trusted. Nana laughed because Pops was talking about her. But she never stopped Pops from putting it on his food the way Samantha just did to Brian. Brian stopped doing a lot of things once Samantha came around. He doesn't wear his worn-out T-shirts or keep his hair over his eyes. I'm pretty sure he even brushes his teeth regularly. The last one I can understand, but why does Samantha care what Brian eats or wears? If I liked a boy enough to want to date him, I would want him to wear and eat what he liked; I wouldn't be dating him because of his culinary or wardrobe choices. I'd hope it was because I liked hanging out with him and wanted to hang out more. Kind of like Will, but not Will, because I could never date him. That would be weird.

Dad builds the fire, and Samantha gets up to help me put the dirty plates in the sink. We leave a plate for Mom on the counter.

I start to place the things for s'mores onto a tray to carry outside.

"What cute bowls," Samantha says.

I'd rather not go into the history behind them; I don't want to get upset in front of Samantha.

"Thanks," I reply, and smile before I follow her back outside.

Josh runs around the yard with Will's younger brother, Michael, catching lightning bugs while James hits a puck into a net on a concrete slab Dad poured for him last summer, after he hit the puck into the sliding back door and cracked the glass.

Will and I are always looking for ways to hide from all the noise. Which is why a tree house would be perfect. Dad's easy to talk to, easier than talking to Mom, since she's always trying to turn every conversation into something deeper, with more meaning. But we've already tried to build a tree house before, so this time we need a solid proposition before asking Dad for help.

Dad's the first to put a marshmallow into the fire. "Mm-mmm. Smelling good over here." He says it loudly and super exaggeratedly to get everyone's attention; it works. The boys stop running around and scramble over to the fire.

"Where are the graham crackers?" James asks, holding his hand under his droopy marshmallow.

"Alex, I told you they were in the car," Brian says,

handing his marshmallow to Samantha. "Can't you do anything?"

"I told you to go get them. I got everything else."

"Hey," Dad says in his deep voice that makes the outside of my ears tingle. "Brian, get the graham crackers from your car."

Brian huffs off like he was asked to go bake a batch from scratch.

Dad helps Josh and Michael hold their marshmallows up away from the flame so they don't catch fire before Brian makes it back.

"Here." Brian sets the crackers down on the table. He doesn't even bother to open them. "I used my discount and paid with my own money, by the way."

"Ewww," Josh squeals. "Those taste like dirt. I like the ones with the bear."

I couldn't agree more, but only a six-year-old can get away with whining. I grab the box and quickly pass the boys half a graham cracker. Dad nods a thank-you to me.

Even though I don't like marshmallows, I do love roasting them. I make one for Josh after his burns to a crisp, and then James grabs my second one without asking. Just as I'm starting my third marshmallow, Will runs over.

He slides in next to me, shoving two marshmallows into his mouth, and roasts another.

"Looks delicious," I say, knowing he won't catch the sarcasm.

Will nods and tries to say something, but a big line of drool spills out of his mouth. He uses the bottom of his shirt to wipe it away.

"Joshie, how many have you had?" Mom asks, joining us. She has finally taken off her blazer, which means she's "off duty."

Josh giggles and says two, when he's really had at least five, before he and Michael run off.

"Here you go." I pass Dad a perfectly roasted marshmallow with the teeniest bit of char, just the way he likes it.

"Perfecto!" he says with an exaggerated accent. He lets out a big sigh and leans back in his chair. "Feels good to rest these old bones."

Dad always talks about his bones like he's a hundred years old. When really, the only thing that shows he's aged since Mom's and his wedding photos are the gray hairs at his temples.

"Uh. Dad?" I say, staring at the second marshmallow Will is roasting. "Will and I had an idea."

He leans forward, his elbows resting on his knees. "An idea, eh?"

"We were wondering if we could use the extra wood in the garage to finally build a tree house."

"Hmm." Dad nods slowly but doesn't say anything.

So I add, "We already have a plan and we're willing to do all the work. We're even going to get jobs to pay for the extra material." I'm adding anything I can think of to make it easy for him to say yes, but I'm also hoping Will can chime in too.

I nudge him. "I can't wait to use the power tools," Will says.

Mom suddenly pays attention to us instead of Brian and Samantha. "Power tools? You two aren't old enough to use power tools."

"Ah. I was younger than them when Pops had me cutting trim on a miter saw. It's about time these two learned." Dad licks his fingers. "I've got some leftover decking from my last project, but that'll only get you a floor and four walls. You two are going to have to come up with about—" Dad pauses and rubs his chin, looking up at the sky like it's a calculator, before saying, "Two hundred and fifty to three hundred dollars for some pretty hefty brackets, railing, sealer, and roof beams."

I turn to Will, hoping three hundred dollars isn't enough to make him want to give up now. "And we can use the power tools?" Will asks.

Dad laughs. "You can use the power tools."

We turn to look at each other, huge smiles across our faces.

Will and I are going to have our tree house.

CHAPTER FOUR

"Alexandria!" Mom yells from the bottom of the stairs. The good thing about an attic bedroom is that hardly anyone bothers to come all the way up, especially in the summer. "Breakfast. Now."

On Mom's list of most important things, number one is a balanced breakfast. She basically lets Brian eat as much fast food as he wants as long as:

1. He eats a balanced breakfast
2. He pays for the crap himself

She thought once he had to spend his own money on junk food, he'd get tired of wasting his paycheck and eat at home more. Almost one year later he's still grabbing fast food at least five times a week. The floor of his car is littered with all the wrappers.

Before Mom can yell again, I throw on a T-shirt

over my bathing suit and hurry down to the kitchen, grabbing my flyer as I pass my desk. I want to make copies before I meet up with Will.

"Morning, monkey." Dad kisses the top of my head, and Mom shoves a plate of quinoa-flour waffles topped with blueberries at me. I know they're quinoa flour by the grassy smell. Mom tries to hide it by adding blueberries, but I can smell quinoa flour from a mile away, even when covered in maple syrup.

I drown the waffles in golden deliciousness before I remember to add butter; I drag my fork through the softened butter Mom has out on the counter and spread it around my waffles.

"Would you like some waffles with that syrup?" Dad says, taking a sip of his coffee.

He's been telling that joke since I was old enough to add as much syrup as I like to my breakfast.

Mom leans across the counter, her mug cupped under her chin, and Dad slides onto the stool next to mine. I have this moment every once in a while, where I can imagine what it must be like to be an only child. In kindergarten I had a friend, Annie, who was an only child. I used to love going to her house because it was so clean and quiet and her closet was like going to a store. She had so many clothes; she even had some outfits in three different colors. She'd let me wear a matching pink one to her purple when I was over so we could pretend to be twins. She didn't have to worry about disappearing into her family's background or being the designated babysitter, getting blamed for something her sibling did or having her parents or teachers compare her to the other members of her family. It seemed like a dream.

I put the flyer on the counter for Mom and Dad to see.

Dad picks it up so he can angle it toward him better, but Mom puts her hand on it so she can see it too. "Careful, I haven't made copies yet," I say.

"I love it," Dad replies.

Mom sucks in her cheeks, and I hold my breath, waiting for it: the thousand questions and her own suggestions.

"'Services'? Isn't that a little vague?" Mom tilts her head to the side. "Where are you passing these out? I don't want people thinking you and Will are going to clean their gutters or go inside their houses. Plus, you didn't include a fee. You should, or people may try to pay you in canned goods or ham sandwiches or something."

For someone whom people pay to fix their

problems, my mom sure creates a lot of imaginary issues.

"I wouldn't mind getting paid in ham sandwiches from time to time," Dad says, giving my arm a squeeze. His breath smells like coffee, and his hand feels scratchy and rough on my arm. "I gotta go," Dad says, and gives me a wink. As he pulls on his boots, he adds, "Alex, you pass those out and charge ten bucks an hour. Ask them what they need done and add that it can be anything but services that require ladders and power tools."

Mom opens her mouth like she has more to add, but Dad puts up his hand. "They'll be fine, Juliet."

Before Mom or Dad can say anything else, Brian shuffles into the kitchen, scoots the stool louder than necessary, and starts talking about the only thing he ever talks about—his job. Mom grabs him a plate and pushes his hair out of his face.

"Mo-om," he says, but doesn't bat her hand away.

James and Josh pile in next, practically on top of each other. Josh hugs a video game against his chest as James reaches over him. "It's still my turn."

Mom grabs the game from Josh and stares at them. She doesn't even have to say it before they both grab their plates and sit down. Without asking or waiting for me to be finished with breakfast, Josh starts to climb up my stool, and suddenly I'm standing at the end of the counter.

Mom cuts up Josh's waffle as I shove the last few soggy bites of mine into my mouth. I need to get the copies ready and slip out before she finds a chore for me.

"Alex," Mom calls, not taking her eyes off Josh's plate. "I need you to look at those forms by the fridge. Babysitting classes start in two weeks."

I nod and hurry toward her office to make copies, ignoring the forms. There is no time for babysitting classes this summer. Not only because I have enough experience with my own brothers, but now Will and I have money to make and a tree house to build.

And babysitting is not the way I plan to earn my money. Anyone with three brothers gets it.

Thankfully, Josh spills his orange juice across the counter and Mom can't say any more about it.

My hands begin to sweat from the heat, and the spot where I'm holding the flyers puckers.

Will had better hurry or these flyers will turn floppy and no one will hire us. I'm about to stomp across his yard and grab him when he pushes out his front door, his towel slung over his shoulder as he shoves a muffin into his face.

Will's hair is slicked back, and I can't tell if it's wet or slimy from gel, like the way Brian's looks when he and Samantha go to school dances.

"Morning," he says, spraying me with crumbs.

The only thing stopping me from yelling at him is the other muffin that he holds out for me.

"Thanks," I say. Will's mom bakes the best muffins. This one is blueberry and still warm. I wave the flyers in front of him. "We're in business."

"Are we putting them in the neighbors' mailboxes?" he asks, rolling his bike down the driveway.

"No," I say. "We need to knock on people's door. Customers like to see who they're hiring."

Having three brothers, I'm used to being questioned and doubted. Once the three of them argued with me over my middle name. But Will—he always accepts what I say, like I'm smart and know what I'm talking about.

"Okay, well, I was thinking last night, and I know the perfect place to start," Will says, hopping onto his bike.

I place the flyers in the fold of my swimming towel inside my pool bag, excited that Will actually gave this plan some thought.

"Great!" I reply, and swing my leg over my bike and pedal behind him.

We ride past our elementary school. It looks so small now that we've been at the middle school for two years. This familiar ride gives me time to eat my muffin. Will keeps pedaling past the school and toward the main road that runs straight through town—the road we're not allowed to cross.

"Will!" I yell.

He slows but doesn't stop.

When we get to the intersection, the light turns red and he's forced to pause next to me.

"Where are we going?" I ask. "We're not allowed to cross here."

Will smooths his hair and tucks in the front of his shirt.

"Why are you tucking in your shirt? You're wearing swim trunks."

"There's a neighborhood over here where my cousin mows. He said we can get lots of jobs," he replies instead of answering my question.

"Your cousin?" Before he can respond, the light changes and he pedals across the street.

I let out a sigh but follow him. We go down a few streets before Will turns left. I'm not sure how he knows exactly where to go. This neighborhood has bigger houses with smaller yards than ours. Only a few houses are small and older-looking. The street Will bikes down ends in a cul-de-sac.

Finally he slows to a stop.

Will pats at the top of his hair and pulls his shirt at the shoulders. "Why don't we split up? We'll each take a side of the street."

Will grabs a stack of the flyers before I can say or ask him anything else. I park my bike next to Will's and walk up to the house across from the one Will's headed to. I knock and look over my shoulder at him. He's busy fixing his hair and shirt again. Does he think we won't get hired if we don't look good? Maybe I should have brushed my hair instead of throwing it into a ponytail. The door in front of me opens a crack.

"Hello?" the voice says.

"Hi, I'm just . . ." I hold the flyer up, but the voice stops me.

"I'm not buying anything. This neighborhood doesn't allow solicitors." The door slams and I take a few steps back.

Will is already at his second door. The man who opens it takes the flyer, and Will gives me a thumbs-up as he walks across the grass to the next house. I stop at two more houses and get another grumpy complaint and a teenager who snatches the flyer before closing the door in my face, so I cross the street and join Will at his next house.

"Oh, hey," Will says. "Why aren't you passing out flyers?"

"There's a no-soliciting rule and I keep getting yelled at."

"I'm having good luck," Will says. "Why don't you try another house?"

I shake my head. "I don't know. Even if we get a job here, we're not allowed to ride across Maple on our bikes. How are we going to explain to our parents the way we got here?"

The door opens, and there stands Rebekah.

Have you ever had one of those moments when everything happens in slow motion? Seeing Rebekah. Her face a blend of confusion and surprise, while I feel my face get hot and cold all at once. My mouth opens and closes, but I can barely breathe, much less say anything.

"Hey." Will's voice pinches and he coughs a bunch of times. "I was riding around and dropping off this. You know, for my job."

"Oh." Rebekah takes the flyer. She stands there, and I think she's reading every word on the page. "Cool artwork. I've been practicing my lettering, but it doesn't look anything like this."

"Yeah. It's pretty. I mean, pretty cool." Will makes a weird noise in his throat.

Rebekah nods. "Do you need a drink?"

Will shifts so he's completely blocking me. He makes a few more weird noises before finally spitting out words in English. "No. I have to get back to work."

Rebekah starts to close the door, but Will puts his hand out, accidentally pushing the door into her forehead. "Sorry. Sorry." He starts to reach for Rebekah, then pulls his hands away and stuffs them into the pockets of his swim trunks instead. "I just wanted to say I'll be at the pool later. And probably tomorrow."

"Okay." Rebekah rubs her head where it's turning pink, but smiles.

As soon as her door closes, I shove Will. He almost topples into the bushes.

"Are you serious?" Spit flies out of my mouth as I hurl the words at him.

I stomp down the walkway. It's made of brick and I can't imagine how long it took to lay each piece in the zigzag pattern they're in. It seems like a lot of effort for something that people just walk right over.

Will jogs after me to where we left our bikes.

"What's wrong with you?" he asks, the "jeesh" in his voice strong.

Will's hair is falling across his forehead now. His shirt is still only tucked into his trunks at the front, but it's wet from where sweat has seeped through around the neck. He looks like Will, but he's acting like someone I don't know.

I let out a sigh. "We're going to get in trouble. There aren't even jobs here. This was all one big lame plan to see Rebekah." I throw my leg over my bike and get ready to push off.

"It was a coincidence, not a plan. I thought with being in a nice neighborhood there'd be tons of jobs." Will whacks at his kickstand with his foot. "Let's head back to our street. I promise we'll find something."

I shrug because that's what I thought we had decided to do all along, and I'm not buying that we ended up in Rebekah's neighborhood by *coincidence*.

"Is it so bad that I wanted to see where she lived?" he asks.

"Yes. It's called stalking." I pedal away before he can respond.

Will rides up next to me, opening his mouth like

he might say something, but he doesn't. We don't talk the whole way back toward our neighborhood.

Instead of thinking about what just happened, I focus on our tree house. We just need to make some money, and our awesome hideaway in the sky will be a reality. I'd even agree to plaster the walls with Will's ridiculous sports posters. Anything to get him to forget all about Rebekah and her bikini and her nice house.

CHAPTER FIVE

I slow down as we pass our elementary school again. Some of my anger has faded, but not all of it. I ignore Will as he tries to talk to me. I wish he'd just told me he wanted to see Rebekah. It would have still made my skin itch the way it does whenever we watch Indiana Jones and he puts his hand through the hole in the wall and it's covered in thousands of bugs, but at least I'd have had the entire ride over to prepare myself.

"I mean, if you think about it, we saved ourselves a lot of time." Will leans back, letting his arms dangle at his sides as he pedals.

Everything about him has changed since we left Rebekah's neighborhood. While he was in front of her, he could barely get words to come out of his mouth. Now he's riding his bike without hands and speaking like his entire plan was to make a complete fool of himself just to prove we needed to get jobs in our own neighborhood.

Watching Will fall all over himself for some girl reminds me of how Brian used to act when Samantha first started hanging around. He could barely eat in front of her and yelled at everyone in the family to clean up and stop being so loud before she'd arrive. The last thing I want is for Will to change for a girl who'll probably ditch him once school starts. It's not like she's ever spoken to us up until yesterday.

Will turns two streets early and waves me along a smaller road we don't usually cut across. "I have a good feeling about this, Alex." He slows down, giving me no choice but to ride alongside him. "Look there." He skids to a stop in front of a house with the greenest grass I've ever seen and the most perfect flowers spilling out of containers around the sidewalk and lining the walkway to the house.

Will nods at an old lady pulling plastic shopping bags out of her car. "Let's help her."

He hops off his bike and pushes it into the lady's driveway. I follow. "Morning. Can we help?" Will asks.

She's halfway in the car, a few bags in line behind her. She pulls two more out of the back seat and looks over at Will and me. "Morning, dears. Sorry about this mess." She drops the bags onto the ground and wipes her forehead.

I hold out a flyer. She takes it and immediately starts fanning herself with it. Loose gray hairs that have fallen out of her bun move back and forth as the paper waves in front of her face.

"We were just going around the neighborhood offering our services for the summer." I point at the flyer, but now she's got her eyes closed and her head back toward the sky, waving our flyer faster.

"We could weed or mow," I offer.

She opens her eyes and shakes her head at the yard. "Dears, this is all synthetic. The flowers, the grass. All of it. My Howard was allergic."

"Is Howard your dog?" Will asks, rolling his bike back a few inches.

I'd elbow him, but he's too far away.

The woman laughs and shakes her head. "No. Howard *was* my husband, as in he's no longer with us. I couldn't even have a bouquet at our wedding."

"Oh, I'm sorry," Will mumbles.

"Nothing to be sorry for. Now, what did you two say your names were?"

"I'm Alex and this is Will."

"I'm Ms. Tanner and I'm thirsty. Why don't you

each grab a few bags and follow me inside. Let's get something nice to drink."

Will and I loop bags up and down our arms. They aren't heavy, but there are lots of them and they're overflowing with scratchy, stiff fabric.

The sun has gotten higher and it's hot. I'm looking forward to cooling down with the help of Ms. Tanner's air-conditioning, but as we step through the front door, it's dark and hotter than it was outside.

Will lets out a little gasp like he's trying to catch his breath. The air is thick and reminds me of trapped heat inside a car.

"Sorry, dears. I forgot to mention, my air-conditioning broke. Just put the bags over by the sewing table there."

We place them down on the floor, and I notice two empty clothing racks on wheels against the wall.

"Make yourselves comfortable," Ms. Tanner calls from the kitchen.

Two pink-and-white floral couches with green velvet throw cushions are in an L shape in the front room we walked through. Just looking at the fabric makes my legs itch. Will plops down before I can tell her no thank you and whisk him out. My mom specifically said to not go inside anyone's house.

I sit across from Will at the absolute edge of the couch. "We should go," I whisper.

"Why? Old ladies always have good cookies." He leans back onto the couch and starts to put his feet up on the coffee table.

"Will!" I stare at his feet.

"Okay, okay." He puts his legs down and starts to tap his foot.

My breath comes out louder and with more of a huff than I meant it to. Will doesn't usually get on my nerves so much, but the last thing I want to do right now is sit across from him and pretend things are fine when I'm still mad about earlier.

"Here we go." Ms. Tanner comes around the corner from the kitchen, carrying a silver tray with a pink floral teapot and matching cups.

"Have as much sugar as you'd like," she says, taking the lid off a small container filled with sugar cubes.

Will plops three cubes into his tiny teacup, and Ms. Tanner pours hot tea into it. Hot. Tea.

I can barely hold the cup as it makes my upper lip and nose sweat, but I manage to say thank you and use my manners, unlike Will, who stirs and then slurps loudly. I never noticed just how gross he can be. Or maybe his grossness just never bothered me the way it does today.

"Don't be shy." Ms. Tanner holds a plate of cookies up from the tray toward me. "Help yourselves." Will grabs a handful and I take one. It almost falls apart in my hand, it's so soft from the heat in the house. Will eats his like they taste as good as his mom's muffins. Sometimes I wonder if he has taste buds.

Ms. Tanner pours herself a cup of tea and sits next to me, finally holding out the flyer I gave her outside. "Well, now. You two are looking for jobs. You're in luck! I've got the July Jamboree coming up and am in charge of all the square dance costumes. I could really use help with some little projects around here so I can focus on sewing the dresses."

I'm not sure if this is a good idea. Her house is so hot, I feel like I'm going to faint, but Will nods eagerly as he grabs the rest of the cookies.

"I've got some painting that needs to be done outside. How's that sound to start?" Ms. Tanner asks.

"Great," I say.

"Five dollars an hour," Will adds. The heat must be affecting his memory. I told him Dad said ten dollars an hour before we left. It's going to take us years to build our tree house with that rate!

"Let's make it an even eight dollars an hour and all

the tea and cookies you want," Ms. Tanner says, and smiles.

. . .

Will pushes his bike next to me and attempts to whistle a song that must sound pretty good in his head, because he's still smiling. The same irritating smile he's worn since we left Rebekah's neighborhood.

I open my mouth to tell him to snap out of it. All he did was mention to Rebekah he'd be at the pool—it wasn't like she confessed her love to him. Instead I say, "We agreed on ten dollars an hour. Why'd you say five?"

"But we got eight dollars plus cookies," Will says. Like soggy cookies and hot tea make up for the difference.

The pool is just ahead, and I'm glad we're walking our bikes. Now that we're here, I'm not in any rush to be at the pool. I'm half afraid Rebekah will be there waiting to ruin my afternoon again. But the other half is afraid she won't come and Will won't be as fun as usual.

"I say we hit the Bransons' and all the houses in our half of the neighborhood tomorrow." He reaches over and punches me in the arm. "Don't worry. Eight bucks an hour for just one job. We'll have three hundred dollars before you know it."

Will does his happy shuffle that's part skipping, part dancing, with one arm moving in a circle like he's stirring a pot of soup, since he's holding his bike with the other.

I can't help it; a smile breaks across my face.

In that moment I know it doesn't matter if Rebekah shows up or not, because the upside of Will's optimism is that he hasn't forgotten about our tree house. And more jobs means more time together.

CHAPTER SIX

The next morning the sun is bright. Will and I already have one summer job. And Rebekah never showed up at the pool yesterday. We played three rounds of Deep-Sea Diver, and Will's mom even let us have the leftover pizza at closing.

We meet up early to pass out more flyers before heading to the pool. Will leaves his bike and bag next to mine in the driveway and we walk next door to the Bransons'.

Will holds the flyer as I knock on their door. Mr. and Mrs. Branson live in Florida all winter but come back to Illinois for the summer. Mrs. Branson answers. "Hello, you two."

"Good morning, Mrs. Branson," Will says, holding out the flyer.

She takes it, looking it over.

"Will and I are trying to find some jobs this

summer. Do you need any help around the house or outside in the yard?"

"Well, my Bob hurt his knee at our last tennis tournament, and we hired some high school boys to mow and weed every week. I'm afraid there's not much else that needs getting done at the moment, but I'll keep your flyer in case something comes up."

"Thanks," I say, hoping it sounds like I mean it. I've helped James sell enough popcorn for his hockey team to know that she's just being nice without having to say no.

We hop onto our bikes and stop at several more houses. Everyone takes our flyers, but no one has any jobs for us. By the time we get to the end of our block, the only house we haven't stopped at is Mr. Edwards's.

Mr. Edwards has a big house. The siding is gray, but I'm never sure if it was painted that color or it's become that color over the years.

It's not just the house that's big. Mr. Edwards's dog is gigantic. Will won't ever admit it, but he's afraid of dogs. Even little yappy ones. He uses the fact that he once had a dog to try to prove he isn't afraid, but I'm the only one who knows the truth: He was afraid of his own dog, too.

"Let's just leave a flyer in his mailbox," Will says. His voice is high and tight like he's sucked on a helium balloon.

"No one pays attention to flyers in the mail. Plus, we haven't gotten a single job this morning."

Will stands at the mailbox, shaking his head, and crosses his arms in front of his chest.

"Come on, Will. For the tree house."

Will lets out a long groan but nods and follows me up the walkway. I kick a shredded plastic ball out of the way and notice a few more plastic dog toys littering the yard. At the top of the steps, I hesitate before ringing the doorbell just above a BEWARE OF DOG sign.

I turn and give Will a smile that I hope says *No big deal!* before I face the door again and notice streaks of dog slobber smeared all over the glass; the drool reaches from the bottom up to the height of my face. "I guess it wouldn't hurt if—"

The door opens and a dog slams into the glass door, barking. Snot and slobber flies everywhere.

I jump back, tripping over Will. We practically hug each other and watch the curly white hair that's yellowed around the mouth, matching the yellowed teeth, open and close in a mixture of a snarl and bark. The dog's head is even with mine. I can see each narrow, sharp tooth and the saggy pink gums coating the thin piece of glass in dribble, our only protection from getting slimed or mauled.

"Shmoopy. Shmoopy, down!" Mr. Edwards appears and slams his walker on the ground twice.

The dog sits facing Will and me, but he looks sideways at Mr. Edwards and lets out a series of high-pitched whines.

"Don't mind this big baby." Mr. Edwards looks at the dog. "Shmoopy, bed," he says firmly.

Will and I let go of each other as Shmoopy click-clacks away from the door, deeper into the house.

Mr. Edwards squeezes his walker into the gap to prop the door open. "Now, what can I do for you two?"

Will's mouth is still hanging open, so I elbow him as I hand a flyer to Mr. Edwards. "We're here to offer you our services this summer." As the words come out of my mouth, I think Mom might have had a point. I should have listed specific jobs. If Will thought bathing a cat would be the worst job we'd get offered, now that I've seen the canine monster up close, I'm pretty sure both of us together couldn't handle washing Shmoopy.

Mr. Edwards looks at the flyer and nods. "Well,

I'm not as agile as I once was. Bending down means no getting back up for me. You two think you can handle coming around three times a week and giving the yard a good cleanup?"

"Oh, sure. Yard work is perfect." I'm so relieved that it doesn't involve Shmoopy. "We can do that for ten dollars an hour." I hope Will realizes that starting high is how you negotiate.

"Oh, picking up Shmoopy's poop won't take more than a few minutes. How about I give you two ten bucks a week? Just promise me you'll come three times." He closes the door, and it's Will's turn to elbow me. Hard.

"Ten bucks a week to pick up dog poop?" Will says, dragging his feet down the walkway. "I'd rather bathe a cat and deal with hives."

"Hey, it's a job," I say as we both climb onto our bikes. "And he did say it'd only take a few minutes."

"Do you think we'll have enough money for a zip line?" Will asks. "Can you imagine if we connected it to a tree in my yard?"

"Or if we could get there from our bedrooms like in *Home Alone*?"

Will and I toss ideas back and forth. The comforting whir of our bike tires across the hot pavement, the breeze blowing my ponytail behind me as we pedal toward the pool, and the promise of the perfect tree house make even the idea of picking up poop worth it.

By the time we get to the pool, I feel like I'm about to melt. The sun is beating down on us. It smells like summer—chlorine mixed with hot dogs grilling at the snack stall. This time when Rebekah walks over, I'm going to be prepared.

She'll say, "Hey," looking at Will.

Based on how Will acted at Rebekah's house, he's probably going to take a minute to figure out what he wants to say back, but before he can say "Hey" or "Hi" or rush out of the pool, I'll say, "Rebekah, let's race and see who can catch the most diving sticks." I'll hand them to Will. Then he'll have to stay in the pool and Rebekah will have to get in and play with *us*. And I won't be left alone at the side of the pool again.

I'm not going to like playing with Rebekah, but at least I'll still get to hang out with Will. And beating her at our game will feel pretty good too.

But even before we see her, Will isn't completely focused. He's doing fancy flips underwater and show-

ing off way too many strokes as he collects the diving sticks. I know he's doing it in hopes that when
Rebekah shows up, if she even does, she'll notice him.
I'm also looking for her, but because I'm not acting
weird, I see her first.

She's wearing another bikini. This one is dark blue
and black. Her brown hair is tied into a loose braid,
and it shines as she walks. I watch as Rebekah comes
closer. I wonder how she knows how to look happy
without skipping like a little kid or smiling too big;
it doesn't take any effort. I push my hair off my face
and pull most of it over my shoulder, but it's soaking
wet and I have no idea what it looks like. Why do I
care what my hair looks like?

But I do care. And I don't like it.

The good thing is, I'm ready.

"Hey, guys. Can I play?" Rebekah asks, just as I
open my mouth and say, "Let's race."

Rebekah barely looks at me but says, "Okay." She
jumps into the pool, going all the way under, and
when she comes up, part of her hair is sticking up.

I don't tell her.

Neither does Will.

Part of me knows I should say something, but the
other part feels kind of happy that she looks like an

ordinary twelve-year-old girl. But that doesn't make me like her any better.

Rebekah has taken the words out of my mouth, and now she's gathering up the diving sticks and handing them to Will just like I planned. "Will, you should throw the sticks out for Alex and me."

I'm surprised she knows my name. I wonder if she's trying to butter me up. *Nice try, Rebekah. I'm not going to go any easier on you.*

Will throws the diving sticks into the water and yells, "Go!"

Rebekah plugs her nose with one hand and sinks under.

This is going to be a piece of cake.

I've only grabbed five diving sticks when I realize there are no more. I swim to the surface and see Rebekah's and Will's elbows nearly touching as they lean on the raft, kicking their legs behind them, talking. Rebekah's hair is messy, but she's laughing and she waves me over when she notices I've resurfaced and am watching them.

"I got eight. How many did you get?" she asks.

I hold up my five without announcing it to the world.

Will and Rebekah race next, and I high-five Will when he comes up with ten diving sticks.

"You want to get a frozen lemonade?" Rebekah asks. It feels like she's asking us both since I'm right here, but she's only looking at Will.

"Yeah." Will pulls himself up onto the side of the pool. "You coming, Alex?"

Rebekah's eyes land on me. Her mouth opens the tiniest amount. Like there are words on the tip of her tongue, waiting to come out, but she closes her mouth just as quickly and sinks under the water. She swims to the ladder. I can't see her face.

Now I'm picking apart Will's invitation to join them the same way I eat a Kit Kat, the thick bottom layer first, then each wafer layer one at a time. There's something about being asked a question that feels like you've got a choice even if the person asking isn't giving you one.

"I had a big breakfast," I say. Will looks surprised, but maybe also relieved. I know that look because I give it to Mom when she's tired and wants me to watch the boys but can sense I've been dying to get up to my room and be alone, and so she waves me upstairs. I give her the same look. A half thank-you and half *I'm sorry*.

I know Will is saying sorry for leaving me, but he's also saying thank you for letting him hang out with Rebekah. Alone.

Somehow his sorry isn't able to take away the sting of the thank-you.

I lie back in the water and float, squinting up at the sky, hearing the hollow echoes of laughter and yelling across the pool deck. It's like being in space. Or what I imagine space would be like. It's quiet. Peaceful. Calm. Swimming and floating and nothing else matters. Not gravity. Not weight. Nothing.

It's only when I dip my entire body underwater and hold my breath for as long as I can that suddenly everything matters. I break through the surface to fill my lungs, and it's all too bright, too loud, too hot. Too much.

From that first day Rebekah said hi, it's been one breaking-through-the-surface moment after another.

Every year, for as long as I could remember, summer was filled with fire pits and s'mores, pruney fingers and the lingering smell of chlorine; Will and me coming up with crazy ideas and never seeing them through. But this year summer hasn't started off very fun at all.

Thanks to one person.

CHAPTER SEVEN

Mom taps her watch-less wrist as Will and I come through the door. Before I can ask her why, she touches her earpiece and holds up four fingers. I shrug, and she points to the clock on the microwave.

I don't know why she's playing charades right now. She grabs a napkin and one of Josh's markers he's left on the counter with a stack of scribbles.

> *Call 4-6*
> *Watch boys*
> *Dinner*
> *Fridge*

I sigh and drop my pool bag onto the floor as she gives me a thumbs-up before closing the door of her office behind her.

I open up the fridge to find containers of chopped carrots and zucchini, sticky rice, marinating beef, and the carton of eggs, which has a Post-it note that reads: *Fry at 6.*

I can feel Will's breath just over my shoulder. "You're having Korean beef bowls. Can I stay? My mom's grilling hot dogs."

I shrug, avoiding answering him. He's too close. The entire walk back he was talking too much and was way too hyper. I don't know why these past few days I suddenly find him so aggravating, even though he's not doing anything different from usual.

"I'd better check on Josh and James." A part of me hopes he'll go home. If I have to watch my brothers and get dinner ready, I'm not sure I can deal with hearing any more about Rebekah, too. Will hasn't actually said her name, but it's obvious why he's in such a good mood. Before I can drop a hint, he runs out the back door to James and Josh.

He grabs a hockey stick and plays goalie for James. I sit down next to Josh and grab a piece of sidewalk chalk, but can't focus enough to draw anything.

"Do you like my omsicle course?" Josh asks.

"Obstacle," I say.

"Omsicle. Lines are for running and a circle is

jumping." Josh explains all his scribbles, and I draw some overlapping circles.

Will comes over and without asking grabs a piece of chalk and starts to add to the course. Josh explains it to him, and Will comes up with a spiral that means you have to spin as you run. It's a good one. I can't believe I didn't think of it.

Josh stands up to try the swirl run, and Will turns to me and says, "Rebekah is pretty cool, right?"

"What?" We're at my house. Playing with my brothers. He wants to eat dinner with my family. And he's thinking about Rebekah?

"I mean, she smells really good."

"Yeah. Cool people always smell good," I say, hoping it will make him realize how ridiculous he sounds, but as I do, I think about all the girls I pass in the hallway at school. A lot of the ones with perfect hair and tons of friends actually do smell really good. I find myself reaching for the end of my ponytail to see what my hair smells like, but it's just crunchy and reeks of chlorine.

Will looks out at my yard. He's not looking at my brothers, or anything really. I shake my head. He's probably thinking of her.

"What else is so great about Rebekah that you had to run off with her? Twice."

Will turns to me. "I didn't run off." He traces a thick, straight line in blue chalk. "If you wanted to come, you should have come."

"I *didn't* want to come." Why is he making this so difficult?

"Then why are you complaining?" Will does this lopsided shrug. I know it's because of his scoliosis, but he's also just being lazy. He knows he's supposed to sit with his hips aligned and his shoulders back.

"I'm not complaining. I'm asking."

"She's just . . ."

"Oh my gosh. Please don't say 'cool' again."

"I wasn't. But she is." Will's voice cracks.

"Because she wears a bikini?"

"No." Will practically spits all over me, he answers so fast.

His cheeks flush red like a cherry Popsicle stain.

I know I shouldn't have said anything. I mean, Will and I are still friends. We have our jobs and the tree house. It's not like he's completely forgotten me.

It didn't have to be a pretty girl in a bikini for me to feel this way. It could have been anybody. Even though the minute I think this, I know that's not true. Rebekah isn't just anybody. And Will and I *do* have friends outside of each other and I've never cared before. It's just . . . every boy in our grade has a crush on her and all the girls secretly want her to be their best friend. So it hurts even more because she *is* pretty and she *does* wear two-piece bathing suits that make her look stylish and older. And now she's caught the attention of my best friend, who seems to like hanging out with her more than he likes hanging out with me.

I push the chalk harder into the deck and focus on the color getting darker. "I guess I was just mad you ran off."

"I wish you had come with us."

I look up.

"She's actually really funny. You'd like her."

"Why do you think I'd like *her*?"

Will sighs. "Why not? You're both girls."

"Oh, right. We're both girls. That means we have *so* much in common."

"I knew you'd freak out."

"I'm not freaking out." I lower my voice. "I should probably get my brothers inside and heat up dinner."

Will follows me back into the house.

I breathe in and out of my nose as I scrub my hands a little too hard at the kitchen sink. I hate how angry I am that he won't just go home but also how glad I am that he's here. I wish my feelings made sense.

"Did you know Rebekah's also allergic to cats?" Will asks. He only washes his hands for about a second, then sits on a stool and watches me get out the pan to cook the beef.

"She used to have a dog, too. He also died, just like Blue."

Is it really a coincidence when both your dogs are dead? I turn on the fire and scrunch up the foil Mom placed over the beef, super loud.

"Rebekah and I have a lot in common. I mean, who else has the same allergies?"

I throw on the first few slices of beef and shake my head at Will. "I bet millions of people are allergic to cats."

"No way," he says, shaking his head. "Hundreds. Maybe thousands, but it can't be millions."

I don't even bother to argue; the beef hisses and sizzles, and I pretend it needs my complete focus.

It smells amazing—sweet and salty, with a hit of sesame oil. Thankfully, Will smells it too and starts talking about food, and he forgets all about Rebekah's allergies.

Dinner is ready and on the table when Mom comes

out of her office. She drops her blazer onto the back of a stool at the counter. "Thanks, Alex. This looks great." She kisses the top of my head. "Let's get this set up outside. You staying for dinner, Will?"

"Can I?" he asks.

I must let out a sigh, because Mom looks at me for a second, raising her eyebrows.

I shrug. "Yeah, sure."

"Well, then grab some drinks from the fridge for you two and Josh and James," she tells Will.

"I'm home," Dad calls, like he always does as he enters from the garage. It takes him a few minutes to get his boots off and put his stuff away, since Mom doesn't like him to track in dirt from his jobs.

"You really are a lifesaver," Mom says as she follows me outside with the food. "I couldn't have done that call without you."

"Well, I am able to help out more. I only charge ten dollars an hour," I say, half joking.

"Yes, but there are some things we do because we're part of a family." Mom's voice has that tone, meaning she could start in on a lecture if I say one more wrong word.

Dad wrestles James and Josh inside to wash their hands just as Brian and Samantha show up.

"Alex, can you grab another plate for Samantha?" Mom asks.

Brian shrugs and gives me one of those big-brother silent looks that hold every insult.

"Brian should get it. It's for his girlfriend," I say. "I grabbed a plate for my guest."

Brian sneers when I say "guest" and mouths *boyfriend* and adds kisses after it.

"Alex!" Dad says, returning with Josh and James just in time to hear me but not see Brian. "Don't be rude."

"He never helps out," I say, trying not to sound whiney as I wave my arm at Brian. He gives me an exaggerated pouty face that he changes into a serious face just as Dad turns to him.

"I'll grab the plate," Mom says, getting up from the table and giving me her *We'll talk later, not in front of Samantha* look.

"Some of us work all day," Brian says. "So it wouldn't kill you to help out a bit."

"I do have a job. In fact, Will and I have two jobs." I sit back and let that sink in.

Will nods, but his mouth is so full of food that he can't say a word to help me out.

Mom returns with the extra plate. "You and Will got jobs?"

Will swallows loudly. "Yep. We're painting and picking up dog poop."

I clear my throat, wishing Brian hadn't heard about the dog poop. "We're helping Mr. Edwards and Ms. Tanner."

Mom looks at Dad, but he nods his head while he finishes chewing. "That's great."

"You're not going inside their houses, are you?" Mom asks.

"No," I say quickly. There's no need for Mom to make a big deal about us going inside Ms. Tanner's for tea.

Mom nods. "I'm impressed." She pats Will's hand and looks over at me. "I'll make a deal with you, Alex. You take that babysitting class, and I'll pay you to help around the house. Not ten dollars an hour, but we can work something out."

"Why do I have to take that class? I have enough experience with James and Josh."

Dad holds up his fork, pointing it as he talks. "I agree with your mom. You need to get a certification. You think people would hire me if I couldn't show them I'm qualified?"

"We'll start tomorrow," Mom says, clapping her hands. "I have an online seminar from noon to five.

You help me out with the boys, and I'll keep track of your hours. Once you pass the course, we'll pay you."

"Great," I mumble. As much as Will and I need the money to start the tree house, babysitting my brothers is only a tiny step above picking up dog poop. But the faster we buy supplies, the faster we get our top secret clubhouse, where raft-nabbing, best-friend-stealing, plain-vanilla-cone Rebekah isn't a member.

CHAPTER EIGHT

r. Edwards hands Will and me little blue bags. "You put your hand in like this, grab it, then fold the bag inside out and tie a knot. That's it." He smiles like he just offered us an ice cream sandwich. "Drop them into the green garbage bin at the side of my garage," he adds before he heads back inside.

I stare at the thin plastic bag I'm holding and realize this job is definitely worth more than ten dollars a week.

Will looks worried too.

"I'm sure it's not that bad," I say, hoping to make us feel better. We can't both be too grossed out to do this.

"No, I was just thinking about Rebekah."

We're walking toward the backyard, and I almost trip over myself. "You're thinking about what?"

"Do you think she . . . I don't know . . . do you think . . ." Will rubs the back of his head. It's something he's done since kindergarten when he's trying to say something but then wants to take it back and isn't sure how to continue. He starts at the top of his neck and runs his hand up his hair, then back down. About three times.

Rebekah hasn't known Will long enough to know this about him. I have to swallow a few times, thinking about her reaction when she does see him do this. I'm already mad just thinking of her teasing him about it.

Will clears his throat. I'm worried about what he'll say. He hasn't finished his sentence, and I don't think I want him to.

"The first one to pick up the most poop gets extra cookies at Ms. Tanner's!" I run away from Will and pretend to hunt for Shmoopy's presents.

Mr. Edwards knocks on his kitchen window and points toward the back corner of the yard. He pushes the window open. "That's his favorite spot. I haven't been out for two weeks and the vet put him on some new food. I don't think he's liking it so well."

Mr. Edwards said it should take us a few minutes, but forty minutes and twenty bags later we finally have the yard cleaned up.

222222

Will throws the last bag into the bin, and as we stand near our bikes, he pulls a small tube out of his pocket.

"What's that?" I ask.

Will sprays himself with it about five times. The smell burns right up my nose.

"Is that perfume?" I ask between coughs.

"No. The box said it's for boys and girls."

It's almost impossible to keep my mouth closed; it's like the smell is trapped in there. "The box of what?"

"My mom had to run to Walgreens last night and there was this sample pack of cologne." He holds up the tiny tube that's almost empty. It's small like the samples Nana used to let me keep.

"Well, it's great that you'll smell good as we hang out with old Ms. Tanner and paint," I say. I want it to sound like a joke, but it comes out pretty much the opposite.

"Yeah, well, I just don't want to smell like poop for the rest of the day."

He has a point.

Will pushes up onto his bike and starts to pedal away, but I see his skin redden across his cheeks and neck. He can't hide from me why he really wanted to test out the new cologne.

73

. . .

As Will and I walk up the walkway to Ms. Tanner's house, I swear I can already feel the heat from inside.

"Man, I can't wait for the cookies," Will says.

"Eww. How can you eat after what we just did?" I ask. Being friends with boys is like that. Will can be mad at me one minute and thinking about food the next. But he can also be thinking about Rebekah one minute and forget about me the next.

"Because, cookies." Will knocks on the door, and I brace myself for the feeling of sitting in a sauna.

Ms. Tanner is draped in blue-and-white-checked fabric with about four sewing pins pinched between her lips. "Mmm." She waves us in, leaving the door open behind her as she rushes back to her sewing machine. She drapes the long strip of fabric on the machine and sews a few inches, takes out more pins, places them in her mouth, and sews again.

I squirm as sweat drips down my body and makes my arms and hands sticky. Finally Ms. Tanner holds up a long ruffle. She takes all the pins from between her lips and says, "One down, only about fifty more to go."

"That's a lot of ruffles," I say.

"It wouldn't be a jamboree if there weren't a lot

of ruffles." She tidies up her sewing table and tells us to follow her.

We go into her kitchen and through a door into her garage. It might actually be even stuffier in here.

"There are cans of paint on this shelf." She points up high. "I believe there are two cans of Pristine Pond Green. And I'm sure if you dig around, you'll find some rollers. You can start on the garage door while I get the tea and cookies." She gives Will a pinch on the cheek before going back inside.

Will rubs his cheek, and I open the garage door for air.

"You want to look for the paint while I search for the rollers?" I ask.

Will grabs the ladder and climbs up to dig around on the top shelf. I find some plastic paint trays and rummage behind boxes of nails and light bulbs until I finally find a box full of rollers.

"There's Dandelion Yellow and Rose Petal Pink. I can't find the—what was it? Duck Pond Green?" Will asks.

"Pristine Pond," I say.

"Oh, wait, I did." Will pushes cans around and then holds out one at a time for me to take. I put the rollers by the garage door and grab the cans. Will climbs down and we take all the supplies to the driveway.

Ms. Tanner follows just behind us, carrying her tea tray. Will grabs some cookies, and since I know he hasn't washed his hands, I remind myself not to eat any of the ones that his hands touched.

I notice the beads of sweat on Will's forehead, and it makes me even warmer. At least it feels better out here in the shade than it does inside. "Ms. Tanner, my grandpa can fix your air-conditioning. He's retired, but he still likes to do small jobs."

I don't add that I like finding him jobs so he'll be too busy to pack up and sell his house—the only house he and Nana lived in their whole lives. Keeping him occupied might just slow him down enough so that he'll be too tired to finish.

"Oh, Alex, that's very kind, but I'll be fine."

"Actually, you'd be helping him out. He gets bored. He wouldn't mind taking a look."

Ms. Tanner nods. "Well, all right then. Now, help yourselves to some tea and give that paint a good shake before you open it. After one coat, call me to come out and take a look." She closes the garage door from inside and leaves Will and me to our job.

We take turns shaking the paint can before starting on the door. The paint is sticky, but it's kind of nice to watch the door change from a faded brown to a light green.

"Man, I can't wait to jump into the pool," Will says. "My mom just ordered a crate of Push Pops."

"I have to watch my brothers. Remember?"

"Oh," Will says.

Not "oh" like he's surprised he forgot.

It's definitely "oh" like someone told him he had to eat brownies for dinner for a week.

He rolls on the paint super slowly. So slowly, I can see the paint pull and stretch from the roller.

We finish painting the garage door in silence. Ms. Tanner claps her hands when she comes out to check on us. "Sure does brighten the place up, doesn't it?"

We both nod.

"Another coat tomorrow should do it."

Will grabs the paint tray, but Ms. Tanner takes it from him. "I'll get that. You two go enjoy your day. See you tomorrow."

I expect him to follow me back to my house, but Will turns the other way. "Hey, aren't you coming over?" I ask.

"I thought you had to watch your brothers."

"So what?"

"Oh, well, I told my mom we'd be at the pool. She'll be worried," Will says.

"So call her now."

Will shuffles his feet. "I forgot my phone at home."

"Okay, then call her from my house when we get there. She won't care."

"I . . . I . . . I just want to go to the pool and ask her in person."

"Why?"

"Why does there have to be a reason?" Will asks. He scratches the top of his head, and I think of James's baseball team. They have these hand signals that tell the other players what they're thinking or what's going to happen. I wish Will's head-scratch gave me some sort of clue as to what he's thinking or wants to happen.

I'm not sure what face I'm making, but Will quickly adds, "I want to get some ice cream too. I'll tell my mom, grab us Push Pops, and then come over."

"Oh, okay." I wipe my hands on the sides of my shorts. "So, I guess I'll see you soon?"

"Yep," he says. A quick, too-eager, single-syllable word.

Will is off and I'm riding home.

Alone.

CHAPTER NINE

Leaning against an open door isn't comfortable. The jamb digs into my back, but I want to hear the phone in case Will calls from the pool.

Josh and James are playing a chaotic game of chase that involves a ball. They're so loud, I'm getting a headache, but it's also a relief to focus on their noise instead of the silence of Will not being here to hang out with me. Of course, there are other people I could call if I really wanted to. The thing is, Will said he'd come, and if I'm being honest, I don't really want to hang out with anyone else.

I convince myself Will's mom made him help out at the snack bar when he told her I was babysitting my brothers.

Eventually I join them and forget about Will just long enough to have fun.

"Run, Joshie," I say, jogging toward him. He's

hopeless at running after he catches the ball. He stands with the ball between his hands and turns right and left, but his feet stay planted.

James grabs the ball and it becomes Josh and me against him.

"Alex, I'm thirsty," Josh says.

"Your face is all red too." I pick him up even though he's too big to carry around anymore. His legs aren't as chubby as they used to be, and they dangle to my calves.

"Pop-Pop," Josh yells.

James and I turn to see Pops coming around the garage, a paper bag in his arms.

"Well, well, well. I wonder what's in here?" he says, holding up the bag.

Josh squirms out of my arms, kicking my shins as he escapes.

"Let me see, let me see!" He jumps up and down in front of Pops.

"I'll give you a hint," Pops says, rubbing Josh's head. "We'd better get this inside or else it'll melt."

"Ice cream!" Josh shouts, jumping again.

Pops gives James a hug before standing in front of me and shaking his head. "You look more and more like your nana every day."

I bury my face in his chest to hide the tears that threaten to leak out. Pops, and even Mom and Dad, talk about Nana way too easily. Like she'll just stop by with a pie or plate of cookies the way she did before. Before she got sick and spent her time sleeping on the couch in the sunroom or at the hospital for treatments.

Pops rubs my back, and I let him push me gently toward the back door into the kitchen.

I grab bowls and spoons as Pops sets the bag of ice cream onto the counter. "Where are the ice cream bowls I dropped off here last week?" Pops asks.

After using them the other night, I hid the bowls up in my room. I want to keep them safe. Like a buried memory I can dig out whenever I need to.

"Oh, they must be in the dishwasher," I say, avoiding looking at him as I do.

Pops pulls out the rest of the containers of ice cream. There's cookie dough for Brian. James grabs mint chocolate chip, Josh takes the chocolate chocolate chip, and I grab the strawberry.

There's still one container left: Cereal Explosion. Blue ice cream with cereal marshmallows.

Will's favorite.

"Do you want a scoop, Pops?" I ask.

"Oh, I'd better just have a small bite of each." Pops sits on a stool and smiles as he watches James and Josh shovel ice cream into their mouths, not bothering with the bowls.

"You sure you still want a bite of every flavor?" I ask.

"Well, not Will's. Never have understood blue ice cream."

"Pretty sure blue food coloring affects the brain," I say, and I picture Will, right now, sharing Push Pops with Rebekah. The whole scene from that first day at the pool replays in my head as I grab the container, stacking it on top of Brian's, and shove them into the freezer.

I take out two scoops of strawberry for Pops and two for myself, hoping that with Pops here, I'll stop thinking about Will and Rebekah. I don't even know if Rebekah is at the pool. Will could be at the pool all alone.

Pops grabs a napkin to wipe Josh's face, and pulls him onto his lap. "Where's Will?" Pops asks. "I figured you two would be up to no good by now."

So much for Pops helping me forget about him. "Oh, he had to ask his mom something," I say, and leave it at that. James and Josh are heading back outside, Pops still has a lot of ice cream to finish, and I don't really want to fully answer his question. Mostly because I don't want to know the answer, or maybe I already know it and don't want to accept it.

"Your dad told me about the tree house." Pops nods toward the backyard. Josh and James have started a new game with water guns.

"Yeah. Will and I got some jobs around the neighborhood to help pay for it. Oh!" I remember Ms. Tanner's humid, stuffy house. "Actually, I might have a job for you." Pops lives for odd jobs now that he's retired, but I doubt he's ever had to pick up dog poop.

"Is that so?" Pops takes a big bite of strawberry and sneaks a spoonful of Josh's chocolate chocolate chip that he left sitting on the counter. "Anyone I know?"

Pops ran Pops's Heating and Cooling for more than forty years and has met just about everyone in town, so it's funny that he even asks me that. "I don't know. Ms. Tanner? She lives about a block from the pool on Ellwood Street. We just painted her garage door Pristine Pond Green."

"Hm. Name doesn't ring a bell. I can stop by the next time you and Will are there."

"Tomorrow," I say. "We'll be there helping her again tomorrow."

"If you and Will are looking for another job, I've got some packing to be done at my place."

"Maybe." I stir my ice cream for a second. "We're pretty booked up."

Pops nods, but his smile is sad. He knows I'm avoiding helping him get rid of Nana's things. I just can't understand why everyone else—Mom, Dad, even Brian—thinks it's okay that Pops is selling the house. I don't even know where he plans on moving to. I can't really imagine him in an apartment or some condo with a pool.

We eat our ice cream as Josh's and James's squeals of laughter fill up the quiet space in the kitchen.

"Everything okay?" Pops asks.

I start to nod my head, but then remember that Pops and I used to watch *MasterChef* marathons when Nana was sick. We talked about school, friends, and even sickness and death. He was probably the only adult who could talk about death when Nana was sick. So talking to him about Will and Rebekah should be easy. If anyone will understand, it's Pops.

"Will's acting like a moron. All because there's this girl. At the pool."

"Oh." Pops rubs his hands on his jeans and nods. "He's sweet on a girl." We both sigh.

Pops taps his spoon against the bowl. "You're his best friend, Alex. That's a way better place to be."

"Doesn't feel like it." I drag my spoon back and forth across the bottom of my bowl, leaving trails in the melted pink ice cream.

"No, you're right," Pops says.

The buildup of tears is almost too strong. But this time it's because Pops told me that what I'm feeling is right. Even Mom, the one who should be there for me since complete strangers pay her to basically repeat their problems to help them move on, usually pushes back. She always expects me to look deeper and find some problem inside myself instead of just being sad or mad. Which is why I didn't even think to share this with her. But Pops lets me feel upset and angry. Like he gets it.

"Have you said anything to him?" Pops asks.

I shake my head.

"He's a good friend. Tell him how you feel." Pops stands up and pats my shoulder. "You can always start by giving him that ice cream."

I nod, and Pops takes his six-foot-tall frame out the door to say goodbye to Josh and James. I wish he didn't have to go so soon. There's too much space now that he's gone, and too much to think about.

• • •

Mom comes out of her office and throws her blazer across the back of the couch.

"Hey, I'm done for the day. I've got the boys and dinner if you and Will want to hang out."

I shake my head. "No, thanks." Will hasn't even bothered to call all afternoon. I guess it's possible he's home and I could run over to see him, but I'm pretty sure he should be the one coming over here.

"You sure?" Mom opens the fridge and pulls out the ingredients for a salad, and a bag of frozen meat-less meatballs. "I invited Will's family over after dinner for a bonfire."

"Great." I spin the stool around in a circle, letting my feet kick at the back of the counter.

Mom pulls out the big salad bowl and sets it on the counter. "Is everything okay?"

Sometimes with Mom I don't know if she's asking me a question out of habit or if she asks because she really wants to know. Most of the time I deal with things myself. Brian, James, and Josh are tornadoes, ripping through the house, leaving behind messes and always needing her help. I do my best to keep my problems tucked deep down inside and away from my family's attention, and definitely out of Mom's range of questions.

But today this problem with Will feels bigger than everything else I figure out alone. Most things get better after a few days. Somehow this Will-Rebekah situation seems to be growing. First it was the raft; then Will found out where she lived. Then he convinced himself they're soul mates because they're both allergic to cats. Now he's spraying himself with perfume. Who knows what will happen next! He could be telling her about our tree house and asking if she wants to join us.

Mom watches me the way she watches Josh when he falls, waiting to see if he's going to cry, before she runs to him.

I'm definitely not going to cry. I'm also not going to ask Mom for help just yet—because even though this problem doesn't feel like I can figure it out easily, there's one thing I still have: the tree house. It's going to sit right between my and Will's yards. A space Rebekah will never share.

CHAPTER TEN

Clouds keep rolling in front of the sun as Will and I add a new coat of Pristine Pond Green paint. The smell of rain hangs in the air, heavy and sticky, and sends chills up and down my arms.

"Watch it," I say as Will drips paint, barely missing my shoes.

"What?"

"You're—" I swish my roller in front of me to show him just how careless he's being. "There's way too much paint on your roller." I point at the drips that splatter the concrete under his half of the garage door.

I guess it's easy to be in a good mood when you aren't the one who hovered near the kitchen window and offered to do the dishes even though it was Brian's night, and pretended everything was fine. Or the one who faked a headache while both our families had s'mores after dinner.

Will was laughing and playing baseball with my brothers like he hadn't completely ditched me.

Will just shrugs and tugs at his stiff, button-up shirt, looking behind him like someone's going to jump out of the bushes at any minute.

I shake my head and roll paint, creating a kind of contest with myself to cover each square on my side of the garage door with three swipes. Will takes a completely different approach. He runs his brush from the bottom of the door to the top. Every time he completes a row, he swipes at his hair. He seems to be trying to pull off a swoopy look today, but his hair has other ideas.

I want to do what Pops said, to tell Will exactly how I feel. Instead I wait for the rhythm of our painting to get to a *swish-swish* to fill the silence. I need to think of something new to say before I open my mouth to ask him where the heck he was.

A loud rumble comes down the road. It's too loud to talk over because it pulls up right behind us into Ms. Tanner's driveway.

"Pops is here." I drop my roller into the paint tray, and Will and I move to the grass to make room for his truck. He still drives his blue Pops's Heating and Cooling truck.

"I heard I'm needed," Pops says, climbing down from the truck. He gives me a hug and shakes Will's hand.

"I'll get Ms. Tanner," I say.

Pops goes over to the garage with Will and starts telling him how to roll so his lines are more even. I knock as I open Ms. Tanner's door. "Ms. Tanner, it's me. My grandpa's here," I call out.

I can barely see her behind the three-foot pile of fabric over the sewing machine. "Just one sec, dear. Almost done with this hem." There's a few buzzes from the machine, and then she holds up the completed bright blue-and-white-checked skirt, layered with pale pink ruffles. The garment seems to fill up a huge amount of space. "What do you think?" she asks.

"Very ruffle-y," I say.

Ms. Tanner laughs. "I'd hope so! If you'd ever twirled in one of these, you'd get it."

"I'm not really much of a dancer."

"Oh, phooey. I don't believe that. You're young. You can dance." She puts the skirt down and walks to the front door with me.

Pops has my roller in his hand and is painting my half of the garage door now. Dad always says Pops can't sit still.

"Pops, this is Ms. Tanner."

Pops puts down the roller and shakes her hand. "Nice to meet you. Alex told me your air-conditioning is broken."

"Yes, and this heat wave isn't helping."

"Well, if you just want to show me where your mechanical closet is, I'll see if I can't figure out what's wrong."

Ms. Tanner clears her throat and brings her hand to her chest. "Wonderful. And I think it's a good time for you two to have a break. Why don't you all come in for some tea?"

Pops holds his arm out to let Will and me in the door before him. Will steps toward the door at the same time as me. Our shoulders bump, hard. He wipes at his precious shirt like I'm covered in mud.

"Excuse you," I mumble under my breath, and make an exaggerated movement with my arms so he can go in front of me.

"I had the kettle ready, so you all just sit here and I'll grab the cookies." Ms. Tanner leaves us in the living room.

Will plops down onto the couch, and Pops sits beside him on the other couch. He looks even taller on the small pink-and-white floral furniture.

Ms. Tanner comes in holding the tray, and Pops waves his hand at her sewing table, nearly toppling the mugs. "Oh, sorry. It's been a long time since I saw square-dancing clothes."

"You square-dance?" Ms. Tanner and I ask at the same time.

"Used to." Pops rubs his hands on his jeans.

I didn't know that, but there are some photos in Pops's living room of Nana and him wearing matching patterned outfits; it makes sense after seeing what Ms. Tanner has been sewing.

Sweat runs down my back as the hot tea sits on the table in front of us, giving us something to stare at.

Pops leans forward and peers at the tray. "I haven't had a raspberry cream biscuit in years." He reaches for one, and Will takes it as an invitation to grab three.

"They're the best," Will says, shoving an entire cookie into his mouth.

I shoot him a glare, but he's too busy to notice, since he's got a mouthful of cookies he's trying to chew without spewing them all over Ms. Tanner's rug.

Pops gulps down the tea and wipes at his forehead when Ms. Tanner isn't looking. "I can take a look at that air-conditioning now if you don't mind."

Ms. Tanner leads Pops down the hall to a closet where the air-conditioning is.

Maybe it's the heat. Maybe it's the way Will licks his fingers with loud smacks. Whatever it is, I can't contain my thoughts anymore. "You never came over yesterday," I blurt. Once I say it, I feel relieved. It's like a splinter, this tiny, nagging thing that you get used to, but once it's out, you realize just how uncomfortable it was.

Will fiddles with the buttons on his shirt. I still don't know why he dressed like he's going to church instead of painting a garage door in ninety-degree weather.

"I had to ask my mom, but the water looked so refreshing, and then"—he shrugs—"you know."

I shake my head and put my teacup on the tray next to the empty cookie plate. "No. I don't know."

"Well, some kids were there. So I hung out."

"Oh, well, sure. The kids," I say, forcing myself not to roll my eyes. He just nods like he's glad I understand.

I stand up. The couch is too itchy and my internal temperature may have reached boiling. "Why don't you just say it? Do you mean Rebekah was there?"

Will chokes on his breath, but keeps his eyes on his hands, which he rests on his knees.

There's a loud clang and Pops lets out an "Aha!"

Ms. Tanner peeks around the corner of the hall-way. "Alex, your grandpa is a hero!" she exclaims.

I can barely force my mouth into a smile.

Will leaps up from the couch. "Well, I guess we'd better finish up painting the garage door."

Ms. Tanner peeks around the corner again. "Yes, yes. Thank you."

Will slips out before I can force him to answer. I follow him outside. Our conversation isn't over. It hasn't even started.

And it never does begin. Will and I finish painting the garage door without saying a single word. We clean up and ride home the same way.

Halfway home Will steers his bike with one hand and uses the other to unbutton his shirt. He wiggles his arms out of it and shoves it into his backpack that dangles from the handlebars. His T-shirt underneath is soaked through with sweat.

"Why'd you even wear that?"

Will shrugs but skids to a stop just before my driveway. I have to veer into the grass and catch myself with my foot.

Will stares at his handlebars. "You promise you won't laugh?"

I shrug. I hate agreeing to something before I know all the facts. Will puts his feet back onto his pedals.

"Okay, okay," I say. "I promise I won't laugh."

Will sighs. "I told Rebekah that we'd be working, and I thought she might ride by on her bike."

"So, why'd you wear the shirt?"

"I wanted to look nice."

I don't know what to say. I know what I *want* to say: that I'd rather pick up Shmoopy's poop than hear another word about Rebekah or about how Will wants to smell better or dress better because of her. But I'm not going to say that. So I push it to the back of my mind, where maybe later it'll turn into something I can say that makes sense. Right now everything between Will and me feels like a bunch of feelings that don't quite fit together. Like, how can Will feel like my best friend one minute, then like someone I've only just met the next? I don't want a new Will.

Will punches his backpack, making it swing back and forth on his bike handles. Red creeps up his neck to the tips of his ears.

I feel bad for being so annoyed with him. "You don't have to change—" I start to say, but Mrs. Branson calls out to us as she walks toward her mailbox.

"Will, Alex. Glad I caught you two. Bob's been

shuffling around the house and noticed our windows are just filthy. You free this weekend?"

"Of course," Will says. He bounces on his toes like we weren't just in the middle of a serious conversation.

"Wonderful." She holds out a handful of caramel candies, the same ones that Nana used to keep in a glass dish on the living room table. Will grabs one, and she holds the rest to me. "Share some with your brothers."

Will immediately shoves his caramel into his mouth. I tuck mine into my pocket.

Three short beeps fill the air as Dad pulls into our driveway. I smell the pizza before I see the boxes piled up on the passenger seat.

"You two mind taking these inside? I need to wash up." Dad holds up his hands; drywall dust coats his arm hair.

Will lunges for the truck door. The pizza's a good distraction from having to finish my sentence. Will doesn't have to change. His impulsive habits make him fun. It's just that lately, they've been the only thing I can really be mad about, because him hanging out with Rebekah shouldn't really upset me so much. But it does.

As we go inside, holding the boxes, I inhale the warm tomato, pepperoni, and garlic smells.

It's from Goodfellows, and they cut the pizza into small rectangles. The tiny corner pieces are my favorite. I open the box and grab a corner piece with lots of crust.

"Hey, save some for the rest of us," Dad says, walking into the kitchen. He reaches over me to grab a slice for himself. "Go ahead, Will. I won't tell if you two don't."

Will grabs a piece right from the center. We can always share a pizza because he hates crust.

"How's the job hunt going?" Dad asks, licking a string of melted cheese off his chin.

"Just got another one," Will says. "We're up to three now."

"Well, I did promise you both the leftover wood from the garage. How about Saturday we frame up the base?"

"Definitely," Will and I say at the same time.

We both grab for a second piece. Dad reaches to close the lid, trying to trap our hands in the box.

"One more," he says with a small smile, opening it up again.

Will's greasy hand touches my sticky one, and for now everything is as it should be.

CHAPTER ELEVEN

When Mom has something to say and she knows it'll be something we don't want to hear, she has this therapist trick. She pretends to have read an article or heard a great story on NPR, or out of the blue the child of a long-lost best friend has a surprisingly similar situation to one of us. So when I walk downstairs for breakfast and Mom starts the conversation with "I was just talking to the moms from Josh's playgroup . . ." I don't even have to hear the rest to know she hasn't given up on the babysitting classes. Even though I already agreed to it, she's still trying to make her point.

"Tammy said she won't even book a sitter who doesn't have a certificate. And you know that little boy from Josh's T-ball, the one with the curly hair? Well, his dad is a pediatrician and said that poisoning and falls are the main injuries children incur while being babysat." Mom wipes the perfectly clean counter with the dishrag, and rubs at an invisible spot with her thumbnail. "I think it's like ninety-nine percent of injuries are preventable if the babysitter has taken a certified course."

I nod, pretty sure that she made up her statistic. "Mom, I told you I'd do it."

"Well, the class starts next week and you still haven't filled out the papers."

"Fine."

"I'll just put these on your desk," Mom says.

"I hope Brian gets his mowing certificate before you pay him again." I grab a banana and walk out the back door before Mom can respond. I'll wait for Will outside.

Mr. Branson clears his throat from his chair in the driveway.

"Hurry up," I whisper-yell, passing Will the bucket of soapy water.

Will barely squeezes out the rag before sloshing water all over and slapping it against the window. Bubbles fly everywhere and I have to turn my head to avoid getting any into my eyes. I hold on to the ladder as Will cleans the second-floor window. We wash the ground-floor window together before Will climbs up to spray and wipe the top half with the glass cleaner while I do the bottom. It's easier this way, since the water splashes everywhere when Will's cleaning the top window. Mr. Branson insists on a wet wash followed by the window spray, and since he's paying us, we do what he asks.

Mr. Branson sips his coffee but keeps his newspaper folded in his lap as Will moves on to the third window.

We get into a rhythm, and it's easy to forget Mr. Branson watching our every move. I have to dodge and duck each time Will forgets to give the rag a good squeeze, sending bubbles and dirty water to drip all over me. "Watch it," I finally snap. "Don't you know how to squeeze?"

"Sorry. It's hard to balance and remember to squeeze."

Normally Will and I make a great team. We've worked on all kinds of school projects together and have landed first prize for our STEM Fair design three years running. But Will and I felt more like a team before; now I feel like the referee trying to keep everyone—well, really just Rebekah—in their positions (i.e., *far* away from me and my best friend). And

Will is running around in all different directions like the kids from Josh's soccer team when he was three.

The sun glints off the last window as I climb down the ladder. I don't think I've ever appreciated what a clean window looks like until now. Mr. Branson grunts as he gets up from his chair in the driveway. He digs into his back pocket and hands Will and me each a twenty-dollar bill even though we finished in just more than an hour.

"Not bad," he says, folding up his chair.

"Thank you, Mr. Branson," Will and I both say, staring at the cash. We've worked all week but haven't actually been paid until now. Mr. Edwards promised to pay us next week, and Ms. Tanner said she'd get us our cash over the weekend. Finally holding the bills makes it all feel real.

A smile spreads across Will's face, and I imagine him picturing in his head exactly what I'm picturing—a complete tree house with a secret floor panel to hide stuff, and a roof. A zip line connecting our two yards. Maybe we can even install a slide that we can run the hose down and cover in dish soap! But even if we don't, it will be an awesome place to hang out and enjoy *our* summer.

. . .

"Last one. Fifty-seven inches." Dad climbs down and checks that I've recorded the measurements correctly on the notepad. "All right, measure and mark the boards."

Will holds the pencil and I grab the tape measure. We start marking. Little pencil lines on the wood where Dad will make cuts with the saw.

Seeing the boards lined up side by side on the ground makes it easier to imagine what the house will be like once it's up in the tree—Will and me playing card games or lying down, hanging out on some bean-bags.

Dad starts up the table saw, and Will and I take the boards to him one at a time. The saw whines through each board, until each piece of the beginning of our tree house is the right size.

Dad explains how we'll attach each board to the tree and reviews all the safety tips for the hundredth time.

"I'll be up here. You pass me the boards in order," Dad says, positioned up high on a large branch. Will and I lift the long pieces of decking and push them up to him. He then screws in the pieces to the brackets he already drilled into place. When we have about half our pieces constructed, Dad has us climb up and nail the boards to a support beam. The air fills with the sound of our banging and drilling, each beat coming together to create the same thing.

"This'll be ready before you know it," Dad says, taking a break to wipe the sweat off his face. "In the next few days you two will be up here having all kinds of fun."

I hammer in the last nail. Our tree house has a floor. It might not look as fancy as the one we pass on the way to the pool, but the fact that we've done this ourselves makes it better.

"I don't know about you guys, but I'm thirsty. I'll go see what we've got in the fridge." Dad climbs down and heads toward the house.

Will and I dangle our legs over the side of the tree house flooring. He holds the two twenty-dollar bills out in front of him. "A few more of these, and we'll have a finished tree house."

"I've got an idea." I grab the small tool Dad used to cut around the uneven edges that butted against the tree. It's the only tool we're allowed to use unsupervised. "Let's cut out a hidden place to keep our money until we have to hand it over to my dad."

I make cuts through a board close to the tree trunk about the length of a loaf of bread. "We can cut out a little hole in the middle so we can fit our finger through to pull it up."

Will takes the tiny electric saw, and I watch small pieces of wood fly up as the saw works its way through the plank. Will tests the hole by trying to fit his finger through it. It's not quite big enough, so he widens the circle.

"I know what will fit in there." I run inside and grab my old pencil case from second grade. It's plastic and rectangular and covered in scratch-'n'-sniff stickers. I dump out the random pens I keep stored in it and hurry back to the tree house.

"It's perfect," Will says as I drop it into the hiding place we made.

Will puts both twenty-dollar bills from the Bransons inside the case in the box and pushes the lid shut.

The case sits nicely on the thick branch that runs under the board. We'll need to add a jamb so the plank doesn't fall through, but for now the pencil case holds up the cutout wood just fine.

"We worked hard this week. I say we go to Mr. Dreamy's for ice cream on Monday," Will says.

"My mom's not paying me until I take the babysitting classes."

"We do have forty bucks." Will nods toward our hidden panel.

"I guess we did work pretty hard."

Mr. Dreamy's is only open from the last week of May to the first week of September. The beginning and ending of our summer. We haven't even gone yet. Usually we go the last day of school, but this year it was raining that day.

"Yeah, plus we have to go to Mr. Edwards's on Monday. Think of how good a dipped cone with sprinkles will taste after we pick up a weekend's worth of Shmoopy's poop."

As gross as it is to think about eating after picking up Mr. Edwards's yard, Will's right. I *can* almost taste a Mr. Dreamy's cone.

And right then I wish it were already Monday.

CHAPTER TWELVE

I 'm trying hard to think back to the moment on Saturday when Will and I made plans to go to Mr. Dreamy's.

I swear we decided to meet at noon, since Mom asked me to watch Josh and James until her morning calls were done.

I run back inside to check the clock above the microwave. Again. Twelve ten.

No one answers when I knock on his door. I even check the tree house. Not that there's really anything to do up there since it's just a floor.

Maybe he meant to meet him at Mr. Edwards's driveway?

I run back inside to grab my bag.

"Alex, stop running in and out," Mom yells from the laundry room.

"I'm biking to Mr. Edwards's. I think I'm supposed to meet Will there."

"You think?" Mom pokes her head around the corner. "You two don't have a plan?"

"I'm late." No thanks to her and all the babysitting class forms she forced me to fill out after her calls.

"Be careful," she says as I run out the door. I pedal fast to Mr. Edwards's house. Will's nowhere to be seen. My heart speeds up, and a heaviness settles onto my chest before sending tingles down my arms. I'm not sure if I should stay and pick up dog poop or ride to Mr. Dreamy's or bike to the pool and ask Will's mom if she's seen him. It wouldn't be the first time Will has forgotten something. In fifth grade he forgot his lunch so many times, he racked up a three-hundred-dollar lunch bill. His mom made him scrub toilets the whole summer to pay it off.

I'm still holding on to my bike, trying to decide what to do, when Mr. Edwards calls out, "You, girl."

The front door bangs closed behind him as he hobbles down the steps toward me at the end of the driveway. "You and your friend did a fine job last week." He grabs my hand and slaps cash into it.

It feels rude to look and see how much it is, but I can't stop myself from peeking. It's two five-dollar bills. It's what we agreed to, but I was kind of hoping it'd be more. We're only up to fifty dollars so far, not including what we'll get from Ms. Tanner.

Mr. Edwards turns to go, but stops. "Oh, and I got Shmoopy's food sorted out, but I wanted to warn you, he's now taking medicine for worms."

"Thanks." I try to say it like I mean it, because I am grateful for the heads-up, but I'm also thinking of when James got worms at sleepaway camp last summer. Our whole family had to take chalky syrup that tasted like banana. And that wasn't the grossest part. Mom wouldn't let James flush until she'd taken a look at what was in the toilet. One time I made the mistake of going in before she did; I'll never forget all those white worms floating around.

I take a deep breath and head to the backyard, armed with little blue bags. Fifty dollars is that much closer to a finished tree house than before. Will probably rode to the pool with his mom, forgetting about our plans to go to Mr. Dreamy's. He'll show up soon, when he remembers.

I drop the poop bags in the dumpster. Will still hasn't arrived. But now I'm glad. I'm not sure what I'd say to him. I don't want to hear whatever excuse he has for not being home or here.

Any worry I had about him forgetting and then

rushing over and getting hit by a car because he was in such a hurry to get here is gone.

I hop onto my bike and pedal to the pool. The entire way there, I start several variations of the same conversation with Will: "How could you . . ." "Where were you . . ."

But, I also can't shake the image of him hurt. So I breathe in and out of my nose. I tell myself there has to be a reasonable explanation.

The thing is, when I ride up to the chain-link fence that surrounds the back part of the pool, I see Will. Laughing his high-pitched laugh.

I open my mouth to shout his name. I'm so happy to see him not splattered in the middle of Maple Avenue and Chester Boulevard, but I stop myself as I take in the scene in front of me.

Will is smiling as he licks an ice cream cone from Mr. Dreamy's. It's the signature cone with the chocolate coating and sprinkles flecked through the chocolate shell.

I'm relieved he's not hurt. I'm upset that he managed to get to Mr. Dreamy's—what we were supposed to do together—but it's who he's with that really makes me want to punch something.

Rebekah.

Rebekah in her bikini top and shorts like she forgot to wear a shirt. Who eats ice cream and completely forgets to put on a shirt?

Huntington Swim Club is where Will and I took swimming lessons, jumped off the diving boards when we graduated from Minnows to Guppies, where I split my chin wide open in the baby pool, and Will barfed hot dog all over the concrete just outside the boys' bathroom. I still remember the splatter sound it made.

Rebekah eating my Mr. Dreamy's cone with Will, at our favorite summer place, makes me feel like I've been replaced by a more popular actress in a movie sequel.

I click the bike lock closed and slam my bike toward the rack.

Will holds the bottom of his cone over his mouth, catching drips of chocolate and melted ice cream. Rebekah's head tilts toward the sky as she laughs. The sun catches her hair in a way that makes it glow.

I slam through the turnstile, ignoring Samantha's "Hey, Alex" as I push past her.

The two of them are all I can see. All I can hear. Everything else is just white noise.

"Where were you?" The words come out fast, the way you have to eat a dipped cone from Mr. Dreamy's on a hot summer day and ignore the painful brain-freeze jabs it sends your brain.

"Oh. Alex. Hey." Will almost drops his ice cream.

"Hi, Alex." Rebekah smiles. Like smile-smiles. Like she invited me here and is happy to see me.

It's the exact opposite of how I feel.

It's also the exact opposite of what I expect.

It doesn't change the fact that I'm mad at her and at Will. Maybe even more mad at her than I am at Will. Will would never have gone to Mr. Dreamy's without me on his own. That was all Rebekah's fault. She's one big distraction that gets bigger and more complicated, like a knot that I try to brush out of my hair after being at the pool all day. No matter how careful I am to start at the bottom and work my way up, that tangle gets more knotted, and grows from a few strands of hair my brush can't get through to a matted mess I have to hide in a ponytail. If only I could cut Rebekah out altogether.

I don't yell at Will. I want to. He deserves it. But Rebekah keeps smiling at me, and I can't focus on what I came over to yell about in the first place.

I hate that I feel like a jerk for not smiling back, but I'm also wondering why I even feel like I owe her a smile.

"What have you been up to?" she asks.

I know she's asking me this, but I turn to Will. "Um. Well. I had to pick up dog poop."

Will stops licking the melted chocolate running down his arm. "Oh no. Alex, I forgot."

"And it was full of worms." I yank the cash out of my pocket and fan it near his face. "We got ten bucks."

"I really am sorry."

"We were supposed to go to Mr. Dreamy's too. Together. Just us." I want each word to grow spikes and poke right through whatever dream bubble Will's been floating in since Rebekah said hi and planted herself right in the middle of us.

"Why don't we play Deep-Sea Diver?" Rebekah asks. She says the name of our game like it belongs to her. Like she's somehow included in what Will and I do now.

I didn't pick up wormy dog poop by myself so she could eat my Mr. Dreamy's cone *and* interfere in our pool game.

"Deep-Sea Diver is more of a two-person game," I say. "Should we go get the raft?" I turn my body so my back is to Rebekah. So it's super obvious I'm asking Will. Not her.

Rebekah stands up so she's right beside me. "Or

we could just hang out in the water." She's looking at Will, but positions herself just in front of me.

I swing my left arm, knocking her right elbow so her arm falls off her hip. "Or we could get the raft and flip off the sides."

Will looks between Rebekah and me. A huge chunk of chocolate coating falls off his ice cream and onto his leg. It sits there, melting.

"I. Uh. I don't know." Will's chest goes up and down. His ribs poke through his skin, and I can't help but wonder if Rebekah sees what I see. Will's scrawny. He doesn't even have armpit hair. He's a good swimmer and can play ball with my little brothers, but he's not one of the star athletes at our school. He's funny, not in a laugh-out-loud way that attracts everyone's attention, but in a way he doesn't always mean to be. He's nice. He talks to everybody, even if the other person rolls their eyes. And, even if he is forgetful, he's the first to say sorry. That's why I like him.

But Rebekah can't know all of these things about Will, because she's only hung out with him a few times. I've known him my whole life. So why does she even like him? Why can't she leave my best friend alone? There must be a hundred other boys who would love to have her bother them.

"I'll get the raft. Come on, Will," I say, and start toward the snack bar. I don't want to check behind me to know if Will is following or not. I grab the raft, and when I turn around, Will's still sitting right where I left him. On the picnic bench with chocolate on his leg, holding a droopy ice cream cone.

The only good thing is, Rebekah's not with him.

CHAPTER THIRTEEN

Holding the raft, I turn away from Will and catch Rebecca walking toward the girls' bathroom. I can hear Will make his way toward me. His feet hit the puddle of water that never seems to dry up near the drain, and his feet make more of a splatter sound. "Alex, wait."

My arms and legs are warm from the sun, but a chill settles just under my skin. Several thoughts crowd my head, but I can't think of a single word to say out loud. What do you say to your best friend when they keep choosing someone else over you?

"Alex! Rebekah just knocked on my door."

I shift the raft from my right arm to my left before I face him. Will looks sorry. His eyes droop the same way Josh's do when Mom yells at him.

"I thought it was you. Thankfully, I'd already changed out of my pajamas. Her mom was waiting in the car and drove us to Mr. Dreamy's."

I picture Will in his NASA pajamas. He's come over to my house in his pajamas plenty of times, but thinking about Rebekah seeing him in them makes me feel like I've almost lost another thing that's ours.

"Anyway," Will continues, "her mom took us for ice cream and dropped us off here at the pool after."

I'm mad at Will for forgetting. I'm more mad at Rebekah for making him forget.

And she needs to know that.

"Here." I shove the raft into Will's arms.

He scrambles to hug it close before it topples.

"I've got to deal with something."

Rebekah's back is to me as I walk into the girls' bathroom. She stands at the sink, washing her hands.

All those things I want to say, or more realistically yell, like accusing her of stealing my best friend and flaunting it, the way her body fits perfectly into her bathing suit, how her hair looks great even when it's wet, and the fact that she doesn't wear makeup but never looks like an elementary school kid. It all sits right inside, trying to escape, but now that I have the chance, I can't quite figure out how to say it all.

I decide I'd rather let Will continue being an idiot, and turn to leave.

"It's not what you think," Rebekah says.

I stop at the door, but don't turn around. I can still slip away without looking any worse if she's talking to someone in the stalls.

"I know you think I stole Will."

Even though it's now obvious she is talking to me, I remain frozen in the doorway.

"I just wanted to hang out with you guys."

She says "hang out," not "play your baby games." So she *likes* Deep-Sea Diver?

It sounds like she means it, but how can she? She only ever looks at Will when she talks to us. And she didn't come to my house to ask if I wanted to go for ice cream.

"Boys usually only like me because . . . well, you know." Rebekah doesn't have to explain it. It's something you just get. The same way everyone knows who the teacher's pet is or who gets all As.

I finally turn around and take a few steps toward her, and leans against the brown stall wall. The stalls are made of metal and are cold, giving me goose bumps up and down my arms. "Then why do you wear that?" I'm talking about her bathing suit. The bikini. She's the one complaining that boys only like her because of it.

Rebekah turns away from the mirror. "Why not? Why can't I wear something I like and look good in? It doesn't mean everyone gets to think they know anything about me just by what I'm wearing."

I don't know what to say to that. I'm not even sure if I agree with what she said. So I just stand there. She still chooses to wear a bikini, knowing boys notice.

She said hi to Will, knowing he'd be nice and hang out with her. Maybe she did want to hang out with me, too. There's no reason for me not to believe her. And Will's never talked about a girl so much in his life. Not even when he'd come over to my house after school to watch new episodes of *The Baby-Sitters Club* with me, pretending he hated it. The real reason he watched it was because he had a crush on the actress who played Mary Anne.

Rebekah turns back to the mirror, shakes out her hair, and reties it in a loose braid. It's not perfect, but it still looks good. Like it's not perfect on purpose.

Then she looks at my reflection in the mirror. "You could wear a bikini too, you know."

I could. But boys still wouldn't look at me. Not the way they look at Rebekah. Then her words hit me.

That's exactly it. Rebekah could wear a one-piece, but it wouldn't make a difference. Boys would still look at her.

"Oh, I'm . . ." I want to say "sorry." I really, really do, but it's stuck in my throat, making me feel confused and sad and frustrated with myself and with the way things are. Not just for Rebekah but for me. It's not fair. Being a girl really isn't fair.

You want to know what else isn't fair? Pretending that stealing my best friend isn't her fault. She's the one who said hi. She knew her power in that bikini. Especially for someone like Will, who girls don't even look at, much less talk to.

But the thing she said about people not being able to think they know her by what she wears sticks like gum on my shoe; it stretches in my mind, not really letting go, no matter how hard I try to shake it away.

Maybe if I'm open to Rebekah hanging out with us, Will might stop acting so girl-crazy. Even if it's hard, I can try. Because that's what best friends do.

CHAPTER FOURTEEN

Babysitting class starts the next day. Mom pulls into the parking lot of the VFW building. The outside is brown and square with a flat roof. The door is painted yellow, but a long rust stain runs down the left side of it. There's only one other car in the lot.

Great. I gave up a day at the pool to be inside a depressing, empty building. Mom would tell me that if I look for the bad, that's all I'll see. But really, aside from the sun shining, what else am I supposed to notice?

"I'll just go in with you and make sure you're registered." Mom opens her car door.

Normally I'd hate that Mom's following me inside, but I'm actually relieved. Looking at this place, I'm not sure Mom should leave me here alone. As much as I don't want to take this class, it will be nice to start making more money, and even better to have one part of my summer not revolve around Will or Rebekah or Will and Rebekah. That sounds like it's the same thing, but it's not. Will's my best friend, but for the first time I need a break. Sometimes you need a break from even your best friend. And thinking about Rebekah opens up feelings I don't quite know how to sift through. Thoughts I can't place. She's nice, so she's not exactly in the "enemy" category. She also didn't invite me to Mr. Dreamy's, so she's not really in the "friend" category, either.

Then there's the Will *and* Rebekah side of things. Them hanging out. Them getting ice cream. Them talking to each other. It'll be nice to have something that has nothing to do with either of them.

"Hurry up, Al." Mom holds the door open. Inside the building is about as bad as the outside. There's a musty smell, and crepe paper flutters in front of the air-conditioning unit that fills up one entire window. There are posters and flyers for Girl Scout troop meetings, dances, and pancake breakfasts pinned to a big bulletin board right inside the entrance, so many on top of one another that you can't read what they say.

"Good afternoon," a lady calls to us from the other side of the open room. Her flip-flops smack against the wooden floor, and the sound bounces around the empty space. "Are you here for Safe Sitters?"

"Yes, we are."

"Oh, great. I'm Molly. I'll be leading the class." She smiles, then turns and yells, "Trevor, the tables." She sighs and faces us again. "Sorry, just setting up."

Mom nods. "This is Alex. She's all registered." She reaches into her purse and hands Molly the forms.

"Perfect! You're early and prepared. That's two of the three most important rules in babysitting. *P-E-P*." She holds up three fingers. "Prompt, experienced, and prepared."

A loud crash comes from the back corner of the room, and Molly excuses herself.

Two more girls walk in. They huddle close to each other as the mom with them waits for Molly at the table.

I watch them whisper to each other, and I take note of how their outfits are almost identical, except for the colors of their tops. The one with darker hair looks up and smiles. I smile back and am sure if they talked to Will, I'd be okay with it.

"I'll pick you up later," Mom says, and waves goodbye.

Molly rushes around the room. Trevor stumbles

with the tables and chairs as two boys and a group of girls file in next. Soon the tables are set up. Six long tables with two chairs at each one. Most of the other kids have come with a friend or have sat next to someone else. I'm the only one at my table. I'm pretty sure I'll be that kid who has to partner with Molly for everything, when the door opens and someone else walks in. When I see who it is, I decide I wouldn't mind partnering with Molly instead.

Rebekah.

She hands Molly her form and looks around for a place to sit. I grab my bag and sling it onto the empty chair next to me. My library book falls out and hits the floor with a smack.

Rebekah sees me and smiles.

"Hurry up and take a seat," Molly tells her.

Rebekah scoots into the chair next to me, forcing me to move my bag. "I'm so glad you're here," she says. Then she keeps talking even though I'm doing my best to tell her with my eyes to get lost. "I was afraid I wouldn't know anyone. I didn't know you were taking this class too."

"Yep." I make sure my face doesn't form any kind of smile or a look that might imply that I'm excited she's here too. I slip my book back into my bag, grateful that Molly loves her PEP and starts class right then. So much for doing this alone.

The air is sticky like a melted Popsicle and smells just as sweet. Dad has barbecue ribs on the grill. He's wearing his Father's Day apron from last year. The fabric is a collage of family photos. It's ugly and creepy, but Dad wears it as often as he can, just like he wore the tie I painted for him in kindergarten, until Mom finally threw it out.

James mixes up the coleslaw, and Mom asks me to watch the baked beans simmer while she helps Josh out of his wet bathing suit.

"You guys went to the pool while I was at baby-sitting class?" I ask loudly, hoping Mom will acknowl-edge me from the other room.

She doesn't.

"My baseball team went," James says. "It was so cool. They let us jump off the diving boards during adult swim."

"Cool." I stir the beans and feel them sticking to the bottom of the pan in the middle, so I turn the heat off and put the lid on so they stay warm.

"Take the food outside," Mom yells from the other room.

James and I bring the side dishes and paper plates out as Dad carries over the ribs.

"Here." Dad pulls off a rib for James and one for me. "Chef's treat. Just finish it before your mom gets out here."

"Hey, hey. I saw that." Pops comes around the side of the house, the way he always does when he hears us out back. Last summer after Nana died, I'd almost forget and wait for her to round the corner after him. Now I'm used to not seeing her there or expecting a plate of her cookies.

"Dad, you're in luck. Your favorite." Dad waves his hand over the platter of ribs.

"Smelled them from down the block." Pops gives James a hug and then stands next to me, his arm resting across my shoulder.

"I can go get you a plate, Pops," I say.

"No, no. I'll just have some tea. I already ate dinner."

"Sit down, Dad. You can at least have dessert later."

Pops settles at the table, and I pour him a glass of sun tea.

"Mm-mmm," Pops says after taking a sip.

"It's Nana's recipe," I say.

"She sure had a special touch." Pops rubs the glass with his thumb, and a quiet settles over the table.

I squirm and wish I hadn't said anything, so I ask, "What'd you have for dinner?"

"A friend of mine, Beatrice, introduced me to a Greek place. It sure was interesting."

I stopped paying attention after the word "Beatrice." A girl name. Pops had dinner with a woman?

Either Dad didn't notice or he doesn't care, because he says, "She must be a very new friend if she took you out for anything besides a burger or pizza." Dad laughs.

Pops shakes his head, but smiles. "I try different things sometimes."

Mom and Josh come outside, and Pops fusses over Josh's new buzz cut. Brian and Samantha join us at the table, and suddenly there's too much noise and no one's asking more about this Beatrice friend.

First Pops brings over boxes of bowls and glasses and candlesticks. Now he's eating Greek food with some lady.

Beatrice getting Pops to eat Greek food is like Rebekah getting Will to forget about me and go to Mr. Dreamy's with her.

How do they have this kind of power? Pops isn't going to keep remembering Nana if he's too busy eating gyros with Beatrice.

I look over at Brian and Samantha. Even she's managed to change Brian. He doesn't hang out with his friends as often as he used to. He spends more time on his schoolwork now, but he still leaves the bathroom a mess and chews his cereal with his mouth open, so it's not a 100 percent improvement.

Could I ever make a boy want to change? Do I want to?

If change means Pops won't get rid of Nana's things or sell their house and Will can stop being distracted and finish our tree house, then maybe I do want Will to change.

CHAPTER FIFTEEN

The kitchen is quiet. Dad's upstairs reading to Josh. James is in the shower. Brian and Samantha are sitting outside by the slowly dying fire.

Mom's at the counter, flipping through a book. Her hair falls out of her "work bun" in big pieces. She still looks nice. I wonder if she was a Rebekah when she was in school. Mom says she was shy, but I also know she was in the homecoming court.

I slip onto a stool near the fridge, wanting to ask Mom something, but not really sure how to ask it.

"Hey, sweetie," Mom says, closing her book but keeping her finger inside to hold her place. "I didn't get to ask you about class. Anyone you know there?"

"Just this one girl. Seen her at the pool a few times."

"That's nice. You and Will have any jobs lined up the rest of the week?"

"No. Not until Monday." I wait because I'm not

sure how to ask if she'll take me to buy a new bathing suit. "Can we go to the store tomorrow?"

"Yeah. Getting groceries is at the top of my list. What do you need?"

"Not groceries. I need a new bathing suit."

"Oh." Mom closes her book all the way and sets it next to the coffee machine. She pulls back the stool next to me and sits on it. Her knees are facing mine. "What's wrong with your suit?"

"Nothing. I kind of want something a little . . . different."

Mom nods. She keeps her eyes on me, which is how I can see them dart all over my face. I swear she thinks she can read minds sometimes.

Finally she pats my knee and straightens her back. "Sure. The boys have a game in the afternoon. We can head out before that."

By "we," Mom meant James and Josh, too.

My brothers pile into the van the next morning, but thankfully, I get the front seat.

"Look, Al, I know you wanted this to be a girls' shopping trip, but your dad's behind on the Davises' deck project and Brian's at work. Don't worry. We'll still get you a new suit."

We stop at Target first. "Boys, you look around here for a bit. Each of you find two books while Alex and I look right over there." She's pointing at the juniors sign, but James and Josh are already looking at video games. "Books," she repeats.

Over at the bathing suit racks, Mom keeps pulling out one-piece suits. "This is cute. What do you think?"

I shrug. It's pretty much like what I have. I pull out a two-piece with stripes and hold it up to Mom.

"You sure you want something like that, Al?"

I shrug. "Maybe not this one, but something like it."

Mom nods. She doesn't say much else, but her face holds a permanent scrunched-up look.

I wonder how Rebekah's mom reacted when she picked out her green bikini. Did she make scrunchy faces, or did she smile and tell Rebekah how cute it was? I find a few that look like I can still swim and dive and have fun in them, and hold them up to Mom.

"Why don't you go try them on. I'm going to check on your brothers." She starts to walk toward Josh and James, but turns back and says, "You're not buying anything until I see it on you."

I nod and slip into the dressing room. I hate trying on bathing suits. The crunchy stickers they put inside and having to keep your underwear on make the suits look bunchy.

The first two show a lot of my underwear. I have to keep pulling at the bottoms. The last suit I try on has black bottoms that are almost the same as my underwear and a light blue top that fits more like a sports bra.

Mom still makes me lift my arms and bend over and do all sorts of silly poses I'd never do, but she finally agrees. "All right. Put it in the cart."

Mom's not focused the way she normally is when we go clothing shopping. Probably because my brothers are laughing about something outside the dressing rooms. Shopping with Mom isn't ever fun, but I always know that at the end of the trip she'll at least get me boba or we'll eat out at Seoul Taco, my favorite restaurant.

When I walk out, Josh holds up a bikini top to his chest and shakes his hips. James laughs loudly, but before he can do the same with the suit he grabbed, one that has most of the middle cut out and puffy boob shapes on top, Mom takes the hanger out of his hands and nudges his shoulder, pointing toward the big aisle leading to the checkout.

Must be nice to be a boy and only have to choose

a pattern for your swim trunks. Mom's never made them even try on a pair, much less made a face when they run around in only their trunks and no shirt.

It's Monday morning, and I wear my new bathing suit under my clothes. I wait for it to fill me with power. It's not that I expect to have some sort of superability like in a comic book, but more that I'll look different or older and *that* will make me feel stronger. More confident.

"Hurry up, Al. It's payday!" Will doesn't even look back at me. He just pedals faster, and I have to hunch my back and speed up to catch him. My braid is too loose, and I can feel a chunk of hair fall out and stick to my sweaty neck.

We park our bikes on Ms. Tanner's driveway and I try to fix my hair, but Will's already at the door, so I just push it up into a bun and follow.

"Come in!" she calls from the hallway when Will knocks.

The pink box of doughnuts on Ms. Tanner's counter is unmistakably from Sammy's. I should know. Pops used to bring us a box every Sunday morning. He even brought us a box the day after Nana died. I don't think any of us really wanted them again after that.

Seeing the box on her counter brings tears fast behind my eyes. Too fast. It surprises me.

"Help yourselves." Ms. Tanner opens the box of doughnuts and holds it out to Will and me. "Alex, your grandfather dropped these off this morning when he came to replace the broken part for my air conditioner."

Pops brought Ms. Tanner doughnuts from Sammy's? For some reason this feels unfair. These are special family doughnuts. They're not doughnuts you just drop off at people's houses that you don't really know.

Will grabs a cream horn, and I take a jam-filled. I tell myself it's just a doughnut.

"I've got your money here." Ms. Tanner taps an envelope on the counter with our names scratched across in pink pen. "But before you go, I do need you to help me get a few boxes from up in the attic. I'm in charge of decorating for the jamboree."

I'm only three bites in when Will's already looking into the doughnut box to choose a second. Ms. Tanner pats him on the shoulder. "You are such a hearty eater. I should make dinner for you two sometime."

Will's head goes up and down as he responds, but it's muffled by a mouthful of chocolate cruller.

I help Ms. Tanner open and lock the ladder. Mid-chew, Will climbs up and pulls the string to the attic steps, before coming back down. He moves over so the steps can unfold all the way.

"The boxes should be labeled 'Party Decorations,'" Ms. Tanner says as Will and I climb the steps into the stuffy attic. It's surprisingly big up here. We can stand without ducking along the middle.

It's also surprisingly clean. Not at all creepy, since light comes through two of the windows at the back of the house. There are only a few boxes. The rest of the space has piles of quilts and a fully decorated Christmas tree.

Will pops open the lid of the top box. "Clothes." He moves it to the floor. "You think they're her husband's?" he whispers.

I get shivers up and down my arms just thinking about it. Mom was tasked with going through all of Nana's clothing. I never did ask her where she took Nana's things. I'm not sure I want to think about it either.

The next two boxes are labeled HOLIDAY CARDS and TAXES 1980. Finally we find three boxes labeled PARTY DECORATIONS.

Ms. Tanner is at the bottom holding her hands out like she's going to catch us.

"I just don't know what I would have done without you two these past few weeks." Ms. Tanner peeks inside the boxes after we've set them down on the floor, and then stands up. "I don't have a lot more work around here, but I'll call if I do." She grabs the envelope from the counter. "Here's the fifty I owe you, and a little extra just because."

"Thank you," Will and I say at the same time. Will's closer, so he holds the envelope.

Ms. Tanner walks us to the door. "I know you're probably eager to get to the pool. Don't let me hold you up."

We wave goodbye and hop onto our bikes. Will zigzags along the sidewalk as he leads the way, using one hand to steer.

Sometimes I wonder, if I were able to see into the future, how I'd feel about this moment right now. Will swerving on his bike in front of me, wearing trunks and a T-shirt. The only hint of a change is the new bathing suit I'm wearing under my T-shirt and Will's half-hearted hair swoop he's still trying to make work. If past me saw this glimpse of this summer, it'd look like nothing had changed. I guess that's the thing about change. It happens inside first. Or maybe when it happens, it's so small that you can't see it until—boom! Everything is the opposite of what you thought.

The pool is crowded and loud today. The sun has already made the top of my head burning hot. We throw our bags under a tree, and Will pulls off his T-shirt and jogs for the deep end. I slip out of my shorts, but as I reach for the bottom of my shirt to pull it over my head, I stop. I've never worn a two-piece before. Well, not since I was really little—too little to know that one day I might not feel comfortable running and jumping into the pool in one.

Will turns around. "The concrete's burning hot. Hurry up." He doesn't wait and jumps in.

While he's still underwater, I slip out of my shirt and cannonball in before he can come back up.

We race across the pool a few times before we decide to get a snack. It's only when we're grabbing our towels that Will's mouth falls open. He doesn't have to say, "What are you wearing?" or "Are you okay?" His face pretty much says it all.

I wanted to look different, but Will's reaction to my new suit makes me feel exactly like my old self— my real self? Like I've messed up and am getting it all wrong.

I squeeze my towel tightly around me and dig

around in my bag like I'm looking for something, even though I don't need anything. His mom will give us free ice cream, and I never brush my hair. I just need a minute before I can look at Will again. I finally stand up, empty-handed.

I might not be filled with power like I expected from my new bathing suit, but I can at least pretend. "Ice cream?" I say.

Will nods and walks next to me to the snack bar, not saying a single word, but he also doesn't close his mouth.

He slips into the back entrance. His mom waves over at me as she helps a group of boys choose which flavor of sour Blow Pops to get. They look ready to destroy everything on the counter, with all their reaching and grabbing. I wave back.

The table behind where Will and I sit is crowded with high school kids. The girls are in bra-style bikinis, and only a few have thrown on shorts. They're laughing, eating, and talking like it's no big deal.

I realize how silly I look with my towel wrapped so tightly around my body. I let go of the towel, and it slowly puddles on my lap. I fold the top over and wrap it around my waist like a skirt.

"Mom ordered the malted cups you like." Will

puts mine on the table in front of me, his eyes trained on the cap of his Choco-Malt.

"Do you need me to open it?" I ask. The little paper tab is kind of difficult to pull up without fingernails and Will bites his nails down to the skin.

"No." Will says it fast and fiddles with the cap.

I open mine and scrape the wooden spoon across the rock-hard top. Only a little curl of chocolate malt rolls onto the tip. I lick it and can practically taste every one of my brothers' Little League games. Will would tag along and we'd play catch behind where the parents set up their chairs. When we got bored, Dad would give us money to buy these same malts at the snack bar. "Mmm. It's good."

Will nods, but he's just jabbing his wooden spoon at the frozen malt, barely even leaving dents in it.

Samantha walks over in her blue lifeguard suit, holding a first-aid kit. "Hey, guys."

"Hey," I say.

"Cute bathing suit. You almost look all grown-up." She smiles and walks toward the baby pool.

I realize I'm smiling, but I don't know why. I think I smiled because she said "cute bathing suit," but now that the second part about almost looking grown-up is catching up to me, I stare down at my frozen malt and try to dig a hole through it with the wooden stick, just like Will. I slowly pull my towel up again, covering my stomach. This morning I was so excited to wear my new suit. But now I want to disappear.

Will stays quiet the rest of the afternoon. We swim and jump off the diving boards, but it feels like I just met him. He only says things like "Ready, go," and "I won." He doesn't make any jokes or talk about the fact that we have more than one hundred dollars now. Three hundred actually seems possible.

"Mr. Edwards's tomorrow morning, right?" I ask as we ride up to my house.

"Yep." Will hops off his bike and stands at the end of my driveway. He looks at my shoes. "I'll be ready."

I nod and push my bike inside the garage. Only Brian's car is there, so I slip into the downstairs bathroom. I stand in front of the sink and pull off my shirt. I twist left and right and try to look at myself from different angles. It wasn't Samantha's reaction that bothered me the most. Will couldn't even look at me. It's not like I wanted him to act the way he does about Rebekah, but he could have at least been normal.

I don't know why I expected a bikini to suddenly

turn me into a girl like Rebekah. Now I feel dumb even thinking of the idea.

I let out a sigh, just as the bathroom door flies open.

"What the heck, Brian?" I hold my shirt up close to my chest.

Brian lets out a laugh. "Your top's a bit loose, don't you think?"

"You're not funny." I shove Brian hard as I push past him. His laugh follows me all the way up to my bedroom.

CHAPTER SIXTEEN

Will weaves and circles around me as we bike over to Mr. Edwards's on Tuesday morning.

He's back to his old self and even looks at me when he says, "We should build more of the tree house soon. All we have is a floor."

I feel my neck relax as Will talks about the tree house. My muscles have gotten into the habit of scrunching up for the first few minutes we're together. "I'd rather wait and buy everything we need so we can build it without having to keep adding a little at a time."

"We've got more than a hundred dollars." Will says "hundred" like it's a million.

"Once we have about a hundred more, we can ask my dad to take us shopping."

Will circles me again. "I have to work at the snack bar. My mom said it's to pay off all the free ice cream. So I'll be working for free this afternoon."

"I guess we have had a lot of ice cream."

"Yeah. Just stinks."

I nod in agreement. Just because parents make sense sometimes doesn't mean we have to like it.

Mr. Edwards is trying to shove Shmoopy into the back seat of his car as Will and I ride up to the driveway. Will stops by the mailbox, waiting behind it with his bike like it'll protect him if Shmoopy breaks loose.

I'm not a fan of getting slobbered on, but it's kind of painful to watch Mr. Edwards struggle with such a huge dog.

Shmoopy sees us and starts yelping. His mouth half opens in quick snaps to let the yelps out, but I can still see strings of slobber stretch from his gums and teeth.

Mr. Edwards lets out a grunt and twists so he's now using his shoulder to keep more than half of Shmoopy in the car.

I drop my bike in the grass and jog over, then hover behind Mr. Edwards. I'm not really sure what to do, but I know I should at least try. "Grab his *T-R-E-A-T-S*," Mr. Edwards says, jutting his chin toward the garage.

I run into the garage and grab the container of treats that's the size of a jumbo box of cereal and labeled BONE-APPÉTIT, BIG TASTE FOR BIG DOGS. I bring the entire box back with me to the car and shove my arm in to pull one out. Mr. Edwards shakes his head. "I can't grab it, or he'll push around me. Just hold it out to his nose, then throw it onto the back seat."

I take a deep breath and walk forward, close enough so when I hold the treat out, it'll touch Shmoopy's nose. "Nice doggy. Good boy." I wiggle the treat gently and then toss it behind the dog's large torso. The thing is, Shmoopy's smart. He doesn't want just one treat. Instead of lunging for the one at the back of the car, Shmoopy lunges right at the box in my arms. I fall backward onto my butt before rolling onto my back against the hard driveway, and bone-shaped treats scatter all over the ground. Shmoopy stands over me and licks up every last one of them. In between he licks my face in thanks for spilling them all. My nose is filled with the vitamin-like smell of the treats and dog breath.

"Shmoopy, no!" Will's voice is loud and strong.

Shmoopy whines and then sits—right on me. A long string of drool falls out of his mouth and slowly but steadily drops right onto my chest, soaking my shirt before running up my neck.

"Shmoopy, off." Mr. Edwards leans onto his knees,

huffing and puffing for breath. "Car. Now."

Shmoopy gives me one last lick before turning and jumping right into the back seat like it was just that easy all along.

Mr. Edwards slams the door shut and turns to me. "Thank you, Alexandria. I owe you. Next time you two are here, knock on the door and you get a bonus." He pulls his car keys out of his pocket and walks toward the driver's-side door. "We're going to be late for the vet. Thanks again."

Will holds out his hand and helps me up.

"Eww," he says. "Your hand is completely slimed."

I look down at my shirt. A huge wet spot fills up the middle, and I can feel the gritty crumbs of dog treats on my face. I really wish Mr. Edwards had left us wet wipes with the doggie bags.

We grab the blue bags from the front porch and start doing the usual.

Even though I smell like dog slobber, it feels good to have my best friend acting like himself again.

James and Josh are in the car that afternoon when Mom drives me to babysitting class. Their baseball equipment takes up too much space, and I'm crammed in between Josh and the bags of fruit slices and juice boxes Mom is bringing for the team's snacks.

"Brian's picking you up. If you need anything, call him," Mom yells as I escape from the car and make my way to the VFW door.

Rebekah's already at our table. She smiles as I sit down next to her. I actually thought about sitting somewhere else, but everyone's kind of stuck to the partner they sat next to on the first day.

"Hey," Rebekah says.

"Hi." I smile. It's not exactly forced or fake; it's more like a question, wanting to know more. I wonder, if Will weren't in the picture, would the two of us be friends?

Molly claps her hands at the front of the room.

"Today we're going to talk about behavior management." Molly holds up a glittery backpack. "This is what I like to call a babysitter's best friend."

Rebekah keeps her eyes on Molly but turns her head slightly toward me. "That's pretty sad that a backpack is going to be our best friend."

I nod, like I get it. I might have even made the joke myself. Before. Now I can kind of imagine things like backpacks or pets or books being my friends. At least they don't change.

Molly unzips a pocket and pulls out sheets of stickers. "Each and every pocket of this backpack is filled with simple, easy ways to keep children busy and happy. Because"—she holds up both her hands and pauses, like she's about to tell us the biggest babysitting secret ever—"busy children are behaved children."

She pauses again, maybe hoping we'll break out in applause. When we don't, she unzips the main compartment of the backpack and shows us the supplies she has stuffed in there: crayons and coloring books, a deck of cards, sidewalk chalk, and some board games.

"Now you've all seen my ideas." She passes out slips of paper to each table. "You and your partner have a situation written on your paper. I want you to role-play how you would handle the child. What activities could you come up with to distract them? Remember discipline is a last resort."

Rebekah reaches for the paper and reads: "'Tommy wants to eat more cookies, but his mom said he can only have one. His mom won't be home for two more hours.'"

I think of Josh and how he does that all the time. "Bubbles," I say, without even having to think about it.

Rebekah grabs her notebook. "Oh my gosh. That's a great idea. I never would have thought of that." She scribbles down *bubbles* in wide, loopy letters. "Do you already babysit?" she asks.

"Only my younger brothers."

"Lucky. I don't have any siblings."

It's my turn to say something to keep the conversation going. I should ask her a question, maybe learn more about her, but I don't know if I want to.

"I always wanted a sister," Rebekah says, not bothered by my lack of response. "Are brothers fun?" This time Rebekah looks at me, waiting for an answer.

"Sometimes. I mean, at least I get my own room. My two younger brothers have to share."

"Oh, I'd want to share rooms. I wish I were you. I'd kill to have siblings."

"Girls," Molly says, stopping next to our table. "Let's focus on the task."

"Sorry," Rebekah says. Then she turns back to me. "So what else do you do to keep your brothers busy?"

It's difficult to focus on her questions. I'm still thinking about her saying she wishes she were me. She raises her eyebrows, and I quickly say, "Play a game like tag or catch, or sometimes build a fort with couch cushions or swimming towels."

Rebekah scribbles all the ideas down. "These are

good. Do you think I could help you watch your brothers sometime?"

I shrug. "I guess. It's not really that much fun."

After several more minutes, Molly has each group present their ideas. "Before our next class, I'd like all of you to start assembling your own babysitting backpack. You don't need to go out and spend money. Find things around your house. By the end of our sessions, you will all have enough ideas to fill your whole backpack."

Rebekah has been quiet during everyone's presentations. She didn't comment on anyone else's suggestions or put her hand up to answer any of Molly's questions. I'm beginning to think I've been too harsh, that maybe she is just being friendly.

When Molly dismisses us, Rebekah grabs her bag and glances my way before she stands. I don't blame her for not saying goodbye. I pick my bag up off the floor, hoping she'll be gone before I get up from the table so I don't have to walk outside with her.

She stands next to her chair and says, "Do you want to come over?"

"Oh. Um." I scramble to come up with an excuse.

"You can call your mom." She holds out her phone. "My mom won't care. I live right across the field from here."

Just as I'm thinking she must not remember I've been to her house with Will, she waves her hand in front of her face. "Of course! You already know that." She types in her passcode and hands the phone to me. "It'll be fun."

I hold the phone up to my ear as it rings. I hope Mom'll say no since I've never talked about Rebekah before, but she almost sounds relieved. "Sure, Brian just called and he hasn't left work yet. I'll call him back. Send me your friend's address, and I'll pick you up at five."

Just like that, I'm walking with Rebekah to her house.

CHAPTER SEVENTEEN

Rebekah uses a key from her pocket to unlock the door. I've never gotten home and had to use a key. Mom won't even give us one. She's home, and if she's not, Brian is. Something about Rebekah having her own key makes me feel even younger than I usually do when I'm around her.

We walk right into an empty house.

It smells like candles and clean laundry. Everything is pretty. The candleholders, the picture frames, even the couch and lamp.

"My mom went to the store yesterday. Want a mango-raspberry Popsicle?"

"Sure." When Rebekah asks me things, she sounds like she means it, like when she told me in the bathroom that she really does want to be friends with Will and me. Or she could be tricking me and offering me a Popsicle to butter me up so she can find out more about Will.

I follow Rebekah into her kitchen.

"Here ya go." Rebekah hands me a Popsicle wrapped in white paper and waves me to a door at the back of the kitchen. It's her room.

She sits on her bed and tears her Popsicle open, wrapping the paper around the handle. "Don't worry. You can sit anywhere."

I choose the floor. She has a fluffy gray rug that peeks out from under her bed and covers most of the room. The top of the dresser is scattered with nail polish, books, and photos but still looks clean, like the piles are there on purpose—a neat mess.

The Popsicle is good. I want to say so, but we've been sitting in quiet for so long that speaking feels more awkward than staying silent.

I finish the last of my Popsicle and know I don't have an excuse to be quiet anymore. "Where's your mom?"

"Work." Rebekah shrugs. "She tries to get home earlier in the summer. That's why she always signs me up for classes and stuff. Then she won't feel guilty about leaving me home so much. I mean, I'm not really by myself. I usually have to go over to my neighbors'."

Again, I know I should say something, but I'm trying to piece all this new information together. Rebekah being an only child. Being alone a lot.

"Do you want to paint your nails? I just bought

this one." Rebekah grabs a bottle of polish. When she holds it up, I can see swirls of light pink and some gold. "I've been dying to try it."

I shrug. "I'll just put it on my toes."

Rebekah opens the drawer of her desk and hands me a bottle of nail polish remover and some cotton balls. "Here, you'll need this, too. Your polish will last longer and go on smoother if you give your nails a buff with this." She hands me a thick file with different textures on each side. "Use the roughest one first."

I nod like I understand but focus on removing my old polish. I painted them weeks ago, and it's mostly all chipped off, or I picked it off while watching TV when Mom was busy with clients.

Rebekah is taking off her perfect polish on her fingers and toes.

I start to add a swipe of polish, but Rebekah stops me. "Buff."

I really want to roll my eyes, but Rebekah makes a face—defiant and almost angry. "Trust me. Otherwise the polish will chip easily."

I shrug but do it. Rebekah isn't done. "I know you think it's silly, but why go through all the trouble of painting your nails for it to just peel off?"

Rebekah sounds like my mom. I already feel like

a little kid around her; I don't need her talking to me like I'm one. "I like peeling off my polish."

Rebekah stops and looks right at me. Not at her nails. She looks me right in my eyes so strongly that I don't know where else to look, and looking back feels like too much.

I want to swallow, but I'll move and it might make me look nervous. And I'm not going to act nervous in front of a girl with a perfect room and perfect pink nails.

"I'm not trying to tell you what to do. It's just that you kind of give off the vibe that you're not comfortable in your own skin." She bites her bottom lip like she wants to say more but is deciding whether it's a good idea.

Now I do squirm. The fact is, I only became uncomfortable this summer, when there were things I began to notice, like how I don't like to take my shorts off right away at the pool. I wait until I feel okay sitting in my bathing suit with my shorts on first—like testing the water in the pool by sitting on the edge and then getting in to my waist before finally diving under. I used to wear a bathing suit from home to the pool and run to the snack bar, never giving it a second thought, never needing an extra layer of clothing. I even notice things about other people now—like how smoothly and perfectly their ponytails and braids are tied (the opposite of my hair), or if people bite their nails or have ripped-up cuticles (just like me). Or how maybe Will and I are the oldest ones playing with diving sticks.

It's strange how these physical traits were invisible for so long but are now crowding up so much space in my brain that I'm embarrassed I never saw them before. I feel exposed. Like everyone can see me—and everything I am is wrong. There needs to be a class on how to figure out all these little things.

And seeing how big a failure my new bathing suit was, I don't think buffing my nails is going to fix the fact that I still act like a kid while everyone else has grown up.

CHAPTER EIGHTEEN

The weekend feels endless. Mom signed up for a work seminar, and Will's at his cousin's. That means I'm stuck babysitting Josh and James. I keep detailed track of my hours so I'm sure to get every cent I deserve once I pass my babysitting class. Especially now that Ms. Tanner doesn't have any more jobs for us and the only thing we're doing for money is picking up after Shmoopy.

When Monday finally arrives, I'm so happy to see Will, I hug him.

"Watch it," he says. His arm is inside a party-size bag of Doritos all the way up to his elbow. He brings a handful to his mouth, attempting to shove them all in at once. A few pieces break off and fall to the ground. Their bright-orange-ness practically glows in the green grass.

Orange dust coats his fingers as he points toward

the river. "You're going to love it, Al. I'm not kidding. I saw a tire, and Max said he pulled a sink out of there a few weeks ago."

"What would we do with a sink? We don't have plumbing in our tree house." I snatch the bag of Doritos from Will and take a handful. Unlike Will, I put one into my mouth, without spraying crumbs everywhere. Will and his cousin, Max, rode bikes along the nature path over the weekend.

"Yeah, but that tire. I should have just grabbed it." Will brushes some Dorito crumbs off his shirt. It's one of his usual T-shirts: stretched out at the collar with a small hole along the bottom. I don't think I've ever been so excited to see Will in a dirty shirt.

"A tire swing would be cool."

"Right?" Will licks his fingers, making his tongue dark orange right down the middle. "We just need that wagon Josh sat in last summer when we went to the zoo."

Next thing I know, I'm helping Will attach the wagon to his bike with a combination of rope and bungee cords. We pass the rope back and forth, weaving it in knots, and we're so close that if I leaned forward, our noses would touch. I wonder if I should finally just tell him I went to Rebekah's house. But I'm afraid he'll ask me a million questions about what we did and what she said, and if she brought up Will's name, so I don't.

"That's about as secure as it's going to get," I say, giving the rope one last tug.

Will tests it out by riding his bike up and down the sidewalk. The wagon bumps along behind him. "It's perfect. Let's go."

We cut through several neighborhoods, avoiding any major roads until we get to the bike path that runs along the river. I've been in the lead, but now that we're at the path, Will rides in front since he knows where this junk island is.

A worn lane veers away from the bike trail, closer to the river. The wagon wobbles as Will rides from pavement to grass. He stops under a large tree and points across the water to a piece of land. "There it is."

Water rushes on either side of the little island jutting out right in the middle of the river. The only way to get there is by a fallen tree. It's so big, Will and I clamber up some of its roots to get to the top.

Will's shoes shuffle against the bark as he crosses, so I do the same. The bottom of the trunk touches the water, and little splashes hit my legs like tiny pricks from a pin. Halfway across, Will looks back at me. "You okay?" he asks.

I nod, concentrating on balancing. It's about ten feet from one end to the other. If it were half the distance, we could sprint and be across in about three hops. The last few feet, the tree hangs over the island. We jump down into the grass and take a moment to look around from where we're standing.

"What did I tell you?" Will holds out his arms at the random items littered all over the ground.

He wasn't lying. It's pretty cool. There's a sink and a toilet. The toilet's blue and sits upright in the grass, almost like you could use it.

Will and I spread out. There are small things like bottle caps and broken glass. There's an oar and what looks like a mud flap from a car.

"Here," Will calls. "Right where I saw it." He rolls a tire toward me. Water and mud fling out of the rubber middle as he moves it.

Seeing the tire, I can really picture it hanging under our tree house. I imagine spinning on it and letting my hair fan out behind me.

"Let's look over there," Will says, dropping the tire on the ground at my feet. "The more we get for free, the more we can do something fun with all our money."

We walk to the edge of the island, this time

together, before I kick something with my foot. I use the toe of my shoe to lift it. A big, domed piece of plastic starts to come out of the mud. I have to bend down and use my hands. As I do, dead leaves fall off and I realize it's a skylight.

"Hey, we can put this in the ceiling!" I rub away the caked-on dirt to show Will.

Will helps me lift it, and we put it next to the tire, the smell of rain filling the air.

"We'd better get these across the tree trunk before it rains," I say.

We each grab a side of the skylight and make our way across. The tire is more difficult. It doesn't roll straight, and each time it veers too far to either side of the trunk, we have to stop and turn and lift it so it'll go straight again. We barely make it to the other side before big, fat drops of rain fall from the sky. We run to our bikes, rolling the tire and laughing as we go.

"Grab this," Will yells over the sudden noise of the downpour.

We hold the skylight over our heads. Each drop makes a loud splat as it hits the plastic. The rain mixes with the dirt that coats it, causing sludgy water to pour off all the sides and down our backs.

Even though we're soaked and mud splatters up

our legs, our faces remain dry as we stand next to our bikes on the riverbank. I'm suddenly very aware that Will's shoulder and arm are practically stuck to my own, like we're glued together. Our ears are only an inch apart.

Sweat mixes with muddy rainwater. A chill runs down my back, and goose bumps surface on my arms. Our breath heats up the space under the skylight and makes me superaware of my Dorito breath.

But I'm with Will, my best friend. This is what we do. We go on adventures and have fun. It's completely normal, something we'll laugh about on our bike ride home.

So the weirdness washes away with each drop of rain.

Another moment that belongs to us.

Will turns to me. "You don't have to wear a new bathing suit, you know."

"What?" I almost drop my side of the skylight as I turn to face him.

He looks away quickly. He said it so softly, I hope I misunderstood him.

"The bathing suit you wore the other day."

Heat flashes through my body. It starts deep inside and then spreads. All my goose bumps disappear as the sweat prickles just under my skin. "So, you can buy new clothes and change your hair, but I can't wear a different bathing suit?" I hadn't planned on wearing that bathing suit ever again, but now maybe I will.

"I'm just saying . . ." Will swallows. It has this cartoonlike *gulp* when he does. "You're fine how you are."

"Well, maybe you are too."

Will shrugs. A piece of hair falls across his forehead. He clears his throat.

And even though he's got on one of his fraying-at-the-seams T-shirts and his hair is a mess from the rain, everything about this summer—the weird tension, confusing thoughts about hating or befriending Rebekah—it all unfolds in my face like a riddle. Once I know the answer, I realize how obvious it is. It's been in front of me all summer.

It's not *me* liking him that he's worried about.

CHAPTER NINETEEN

Will and I ride back home as the rain slows to a drizzle. It stops altogether when we're back in our neighborhood.

Dad's loading some tools into his truck as Will and I ride up to the garage.

"What's this?" he asks, pointing at the wagon.

My skin is sticky and everything smells sour. I wait a second before answering, wondering if Will is going to break our silence first. He does.

"We found great stuff for the tree house." Will hops off his bike and lifts the skylight. "Won't this be perfect?"

"Where did you find this?" Dad asks.

"Off the bike path along the river," I say.

"Resourceful. I like it." Dad closes the back of his truck and grabs the tire. He rolls it to the corner of the garage and shows Will where to put the skylight.

"You guys have enough money for a shopping trip?"

"Yeah! Let's go." Will wipes his hand on his shorts and raises his eyebrows at me.

"I can't take you guys now. Just came back for these tools. How about Wednesday?" Dad tugs on my braid before hopping into his truck and backing out of the driveway.

"You wanna grab a snack?" Will asks.

"Actually, I'm behind on my cross-country training. Coach gave us a preseason weekly mileage chart, and I haven't logged any miles since we started working."

Will starts to untie the wagon from his bike, and I bend down to help. "I guess we should go to Mr. Edwards's tomorrow?" he asks.

"I have babysitting class in the afternoon. We could go in the morning?"

"Oh, um. I can't in the morning. Let's go Wednesday before we go shopping with your dad," Will says, and hands me the rope and bungee cords. "See ya."

He pushes his bike across the grass between our driveways. I want to call out "See ya" or "Later, crocodile," like when we were little and kept getting the "Later, gator" and "After a while, crocodile" mixed up. Anything that will make it feel like we're still connected.

Will disappears into his garage. I don't even bother changing into my running sneakers; I just need to move.

I jog away from our houses to anywhere but here.

Rebekah rushes into the building, the metal door clanging behind her. She's almost thirty minutes late for class.

I think about her in her house—with her mango-raspberry Popsicles and nice-smelling candles—all alone. Maybe no one reminded her it was time to leave, like how Mom yells up the stairs to me, warning me I have an hour, then a half hour, then ten minutes, so I'm ready and not rushing out the door.

But when she slides into the chair next to me, I smell sunscreen and her hair is damp. A pink strap peeks out from the collar of her T-shirt.

My moment of feeling sorry for her is snapped right up. I can't help but feel a pinch in my chest, thinking of her at the pool while I was stuck at home all morning doing laundry and emptying the dishwasher because Mom needed me around to watch James and Josh.

Molly looks up. "Rebekah, you really must get here on time. Parents appreciate punctuality."

Rebekah smiles and nods, but stares down at the table once Molly starts explaining what we'll be doing in class.

I keep wanting to look over at her, but I really don't want to care how she's feeling, when Will already cares enough for the both of us. He doesn't even bother to put on deodorant when we hang out. Not that I mind.

Molly passes papers around the room. "Here are questions for you to think about as we watch today's video. I want you to analyze what the babysitter is doing correctly and incorrectly."

Molly starts the video. The picture has an orangey tint to it and everything looks old. The babysitter wears a yellow shirt with a collar, and her hair has a weird flip to it in the front. She's getting two kids ready for dinner. She puts one in a high chair with a handful of Cheerios, and the older one is running around the kitchen, swinging a play sword back and forth in front of him. He yells "Ya! Ya!" over and over in the same voice Josh uses when he's trying too hard to be cute.

Just as Sword Kid gets in front of the stove, water boils over the sides of the pot. It looks very similar to dish soap bubbles. Everything pauses in midair. The baby has a handful of food halfway to his mouth; the babysitter is reaching for the pot or the little boy, it's hard to tell which; and the little boy's arms and legs are stretched in a run. The scene is frozen as we figure out what the babysitter should do.

"How can you avoid this kind of disaster?" Molly asks.

Rebekah raises her hand.

Molly nods at her.

"She should have put on a TV show for them and then started cooking."

One of the boys at the table beside us laughs. "You can't just put on the TV." He rolls his eyes and nudges his friend. "You give them a game to play in the other room while you cook in the kitchen."

I'm not in the mood to defend Rebekah, but I also don't like that this boy is rolling his eyes at her suggestion. "You shouldn't put them in a different room. What if the baby eats a game piece?" I ask.

The boy sighs. "Not a game with small pieces. Everybody knows that."

Rebekah scoots her chair back and looks like she's about to stand up out of it.

Molly holds up her hands. "You all have good points. And, yes, having the children occupied and settled before cooking is important. Especially when you are using a stove or an oven." She stands in the aisle between our tables, one hand on each. "Now, talk with your partner about some appropriate activities you could give the children to do. Then we'll continue watching."

I scribble down *Set the table* and *Color at the table*. I expect Rebekah to start talking, but she's been pretty quiet today, outside of answering Molly's question.

I don't really know what kind of student Rebekah is. We've never had a class together. I've only known her as the popular girl at school and now the girl from the pool who is slowly taking away my best friend.

I bite the inside of my cheek. I was frustrated that Rebekah didn't know anything about me, but I know just as little about her—and I've been to her house. I wonder if it's my turn to invite her over. I'm not sure, so I push my paper closer to her. "I wrote these down. Any other ideas?"

Rebekah shrugs. "It's so scary. I'm probably going to be a terrible babysitter. You have all kinds of experience. You're lucky."

"You won't think I'm so lucky if you spend a day at my house."

"Okay," Rebekah says.

"Okay?" I'm confused, but then I take in Rebekah's expression. Her eyes are wide and she's smiling. "Oh, of course, you should come over sometime."

Rebekah gives my arm a quick squeeze with her hand, and Molly starts the video. It makes a squeaky sound and shows the action going in reverse, then stops back at the beginning of the scene. A man in a blue suit with a white, buttoned shirt appears on the screen, talking in a deep voice. "When in the kitchen, follow the three Cs. One, clear. The path to the stove should be clear. Two, communicate. Tell the children what you are doing." The video zooms in on the babysitter. "'Billy, Tim, I'm cooking. It's hot. Stay away.' The third C is: careful. You can never be too careful. A bonus C is to check, and then double-check!" He points his finger and flicks it upward, and a blue tick appears on the screen.

Rebekah glances at me, and we both giggle as we roll our eyes.

In that moment something changed. I feel more relaxed. More like myself than I have since I first saw Rebekah at the pool—the way I feel after a good stretch right before a long run. Laughing with Rebekah gives me that same kind of relief, like she isn't this stranger stealing something away from me but more like someone filling in the pieces I didn't even know were missing.

The main door opens in front of us, spreading sunlight from outside into the hall.

Molly puts her hands on her cheeks. "Oh, Beatrice! I nearly forgot." Molly turns the video off and motions for Trevor to turn on the lights. "We'll stop just a few minutes early today, class. I need everyone's help clearing the tables and chairs." Molly waves at Trevor to get things started.

There are lots of loud bangs and scrapes as we drag our chairs to Trevor. He tells us to put the tables on their sides and fold in the legs. I'm trying to wiggle the metal leg closed when someone says, "Alex. Fancy meeting you here."

It's Ms. Tanner. "Wow. You look great," I say.

She steps back and takes a goofy bow in her ruffled purple-and-white-checked skirt. "Why, thank you. Just some square-dance fun before the big jamboree."

Rebekah hits her side of the legs in with a clang, and another person I'd never expect to be wearing purple walks through the door.

Pops.

The purple of his shirt and long, skinny tie match

Ms. Tanner's dress perfectly. Almost like they were meant to be a set.

I look at Ms. Tanner and back at Pops.

Molly walks over to grab Rebekah's and my table. "Thank you, girls. Beatrice, the hall's all yours."

Beatrice.

Ms. Tanner.

Pops's friend Beatrice is Ms. Tanner?

She's the one getting Pops to eat Greek food and to wear purple?

The worst part is, none of this would have happened if I hadn't introduced them.

Could this summer get any worse?

CHAPTER TWENTY

om keeps looking at me in the rearview mirror but acts like she's checking traffic. She might not be wearing her "therapy blazer," as Dad calls it, but her facial expression says it all. The way she bites her lips and pinches her mouth to the side, then sets her face normal again when our eyes meet in the mirror. She dying to say, "Sharing your feelings leads to a path of healthy healing" or some other nonsense that's supposed to get me to talk.

The thing is, feelings are called "feelings" because you feel them, not talk about them. The more she pretends to not look at me, the hotter my skin burns.

Mom backs slowly down the driveway, and stops just outside the garage. Dad always pulls her van in once he's unloaded his truck for the night.

She stops the van but doesn't turn it off. "Alex,

Pops used to square-dance, and he missed it. I, for one, am happy he's made a new friend."

"Are you glad his new friend just so happens to be a girl? She doesn't even look like Nana." That's not really what I mean, but it's hard to explain this to Mom. It would be creepy if Pops found someone who looked just like Nana. What I mean is that Ms. Tanner is nothing like Nana. Nana was short, tiny, had black hair, and was loud. She talked loudly, cooked loudly, and laughed loudly. Ms. Tanner is tall with gray hair and speaks softly and slowly. I don't even know if I've heard her laugh. She's only ever served us hot tea and store-bought cookies. Can she cook as good as Nana? Does she like sun tea?

I shove the door open, but we have one of those van doors that takes its time rolling across the side of the car, not really allowing me to storm away the way I'd like to

"Alex," Mom says, climbing out of the driver's seat, stopping me from walking past her. "Pops isn't trying to replace Nana."

"No, he's trying to forget her. To fill her place with someone else."

The words "someone else" barely make their way out of my throat. They burn as I try to swallow them away. The van door slides closed, and Mom steps closer to me. She wraps her arms around me. I let her, but I don't hug her back.

"Look, I'm going inside; I have a client call. The boys will be home soon. Why don't you choose the takeout tonight?" She combs her fingers through my ponytail. "There are hot dogs in the fridge for your brothers if you want Thai."

I shrug. It's not like ordering out dinner is going to change the fact that Pops is hanging out with Ms. Tanner. Mom kisses the top of my head and makes her way in.

She doesn't seem to think there's anything wrong with Pops selling his house, getting rid of Nana's things, and now spending time with another lady.

Doesn't she understand? This isn't about Pops being happy. This is about everyone forgetting Nana.

The box with the colored glasses Nana always set around the table to "brighten things up" is on the floor by the garage door that leads inside. Discarded. I grab a yellow glass. I lift it up and let the sun shine right through it. Rectangles of color flash across the wall.

Then I throw it right at the ground.

It shatters against the concrete floor of the garage.

Some pieces are big and jagged. Others glitter in tiny shards like dust.

My body sighs in relief. I grab another. And another. Each shatter gives my neck and shoulders more room to move and breathe. Eventually I reach into the box and there are no glasses left.

The weight of what I've done presses down on me, and suddenly I can't breathe.

I look at the shattered glass. There are so many pieces and colors, I can't imagine ever being able to put it all back together.

I've ruined everything. Just like Pops, I've ruined part of Nana's memory.

Dad's truck horn bleeps a few short times. I look up as he pulls into the driveway, and stops next to Mom's van. Josh and James bounce around in the back seat. They fall out of the door in a bundle of laughs, arms wrapped up in a wrestling move. "Whoa, boys." Dad looks down at the garage floor. "Go through the front door." He looks at me, but I can't tell what he's thinking. The boys let out a loud *whoop*. "Quietly!" He turns back to me. "Alex, what happened?" Dad looks from the broken glass to my tear-streaked face. "It's okay. They're just things."

My eyes stay on the sharpest piece of blue glass

near my big toe. I wait for Dad to get mad. He always liked Nana's dishes. He said they brought back memories of holidays and family meals since he was a kid.

Dad sighs, long and steadily; it reminds me of the way my breath comes out of my mouth when I've been running a long time. He's wearing work boots, so he crunches right across the mess and stands next to me. "Did it feel good?"

I turn to him. A few leftover tears roll down my cheeks. "Did what feel good?"

"Throwing the glasses."

I nod, and more tears spill out, along with a laugh. "It did." I swallow. "But not now."

"Ah." Dad waves his hand at the mess. "I've got all Nana's memories up here." He taps the side of his head. "You know something?"

I shake my head.

"Love isn't about dividing items up. It's about multiplying. Your mom and I didn't stop loving Brian when you were born. And when James and Josh came along, we didn't stop loving the two of you."

I shrug because it's not really true. I do more chores, and Josh definitely gets more attention than the rest of us.

"I know you think it's just something parents say.

You're thinking Josh gets babied and Brian gets away with things you don't." Dad puts his arm around me. "Each of you is so unique. That comes with different expectations, and if I'm being honest, sometimes things are unfair. But it doesn't mean our love for each of you is any more or less."

Dad lets everything fall quiet for a few minutes. I always like that he does that. Mom wants to talk and talk and never give me the time to think about what was said or what I want to say.

"Some changes downright stink, Alex. Others, well, they might just surprise you."

I know Dad's right. Or at least two-thirds right. Because there is another category of change. The one called mistakes.

CHAPTER TWENTY-ONE

ash browns, asparagus frittata, and banana muffins line the middle of the dining table when I come downstairs for breakfast.

Mom didn't yell to wake anyone up, but somehow Brian is already sitting down. There are two muffin wrappers on his plate.

Dad passes me as I'm still standing at the bottom step, looking at all the food. It's not even a holiday. He holds up his mug. "Morning. You hungry?"

I sit next to James and watch my brothers eat. It's amazing, the variety of ways they eat. Josh enjoys his muffin by trying to shove the entire center of it into his mouth first. He pretty much turns the muffin into a pile of crumbs. Brian balances a slice of frittata on his fork and eats bites from it. Only James eats somewhat normally. He spikes pieces of asparagus out of the frittata and makes a pile of them on one side of his plate. Then he eats the egg part.

Mom walks in with her therapist face on. It's her calm face—not smiling or frowning. No wrinkles around her eyes. "Good. I'm glad everyone's down here."

She and Dad sit at opposite ends of the table. We have ten chairs, but no one usually sits at the heads of the table except when Nana and Pops used to eat with us.

I scoop hash browns onto my plate, and Dad pushes the mustard toward me. This whole breakfast is way too planned. I watch Mom and Dad as I add pepper to my hash browns and drag a bite through the squirt of mustard.

"Your father and I thought it'd be a good idea to discuss Pops and the changes that have been happening this summer." Mom looks to Dad, but he's helping himself to a big scoop of hash browns. "You may have heard Pops mention his new friend, Beatrice."

Brian lets out a long, loud groan.

"Did you have something to *share*?" Mom asks, her work voice matching her facial expression.

"Share" is just another word for "talk," but it makes Mom sound a whole lot less bossy.

"Can you *share* more muffins?" Josh asks. He

blinks his long eyelashes, but Mom doesn't break. She pushes the plate of muffins toward him.

Dad sets his mug down. "Well, I'd just like to say—"

Mom clears her throat.

"Something I'd like to *share*," Dad begins again, "is that this is all as much of a shock to your mom and me as it is to you. The important thing is that Pops seems happy."

"Yes," Mom butts in. "Pops is still Pops, and nothing is going to change that. He'll still come over and be a part of all our special moments just like he always has. And there will be times, I'm sure, when Beatrice will come with him."

Mom and Dad smile at each other like they've just erased all the bad news in the world.

"Are they going to get married?" James asks.

Mom breaks therapist mode; wrinkles crease her forehead.

"No," I say, and then hope it didn't come out as loudly as I think it did.

"Eww," Brian says. "They're too old for that."

Josh licks muffin crumbs off the table.

Mom relaxes her face and says, "James, that's a great question. I think it's too early to talk about marriage, but Pops *could* get remarried." Mom's voice changes, and Dad quickly takes over.

"I think the point here is, Pops is happy. Let's not make this difficult for him. We should be happy for him."

Dad pats my hand, and all I can taste is the sharp tang of mustard in the back of my throat.

I wait for Will on the tree-house floor. As the wind blows through the leaves of the tree, I wish it'd take my thoughts away with it.

Dad's ladder rattles as Will climbs up.

"We have to figure out a way to get up when the tree house is finished," he says, crawling to the edge next to me. "Like a rope ladder we can pull up so no one else can follow."

I nod and hold out my old pencil case that we stashed our cash in. I want to get down to business. Anything to take my mind off thinking about Pops and Ms. Tanner. I'm not ready to tell Will about it. Yet. I'm afraid if I say it out loud, it'll make it all too real.

Will holds out his hand as I slap bills into it.

"Forty from the Bransons for window-washing. Eighty from Ms. Tanner." I mumble her name. "Thirty from Mr. Edwards." A hundred and fifty dollars looks like a lot of money in Will's palm, but I hope it's enough when we go to the hardware store with Dad.

We're staring at a pile of wood, and all I can think about is Pops wearing a purple outfit, dancing in circles with poofy-skirt-wearing Ms. Tanner. Did Pops laugh? Was he nervous? Did their hands touch? It's not something I want to picture for too long.

Will nods at something Dad says, and elbows me. I shrug but can't bring myself to say anything; it's too much effort.

"These are what you need for a roof." Dad points to another stack of lumber piled on the ground. The pieces are taller than him and cost just over seven dollars a board.

"How many do we need?" I ask, already doing the math in my head.

"Hmm." Dad rubs his chin. "It's gonna be about a hundred and fifty bucks."

Well, at least the math part was easy. We'll be spending all our money today and still not have completed the tree house.

"What about the tire swing?" Will asks.

"You two can probably find rope and a swivel

bracket in the garage. I'll throw that in since you found a used tire."

"Deal." Will sticks out his hand, and Dad laughs as he shakes it.

"Why do I feel like this isn't a deal for me? Your next paycheck, you two owe me an ice cream from Mr. Dreamy's."

"Yes, sir," Will says, making Dad laugh more.

Dad lowers the truck windows on the drive back home. Our wood for framing the tree house and the roof is stacked in the back of the truck with a little red flag tied to the end of one of the pieces. Will called dibs on the middle because he likes to play with the radio. I lean against the door and let as much wind as I can whip past my face. I like the way my hair moves on its own.

Will stops the radio on a song we were obsessed with last summer. We belt out a few lines.

"It's gonna be a fun kinda, sunshine kinda day!

"Surf-on-the-waves kinda—out-in-the-sun kinda—wish-those-clouds-away kinda—summer day."

The words are coming out of our mouths at the same time, like we're finishing each other's sentences. I wish we could spend the rest of the day driving and singing. This is how the whole summer should have been so far. Not me worrying about Will liking some-one else more or taking classes in a dingy VFW room, or imagining Pops twirling Beatrice on a dance floor.

Once we're home, Will and I help Dad unload the wood and carry it under the tree house. I'm already sweaty but can't wait to get to work.

"We're going to have to get this framed up first. You two had better put on your gloves and safety goggles." Dad grabs his tools, and we follow him up the ladder.

It takes all three of us to get the framing done, which is basically a wooden skeleton we'll build the walls and roof from. Will and I hold the pieces of wood in place as Dad levels them and shoots nails.

The nail gun, the squeak of the wood as it scrapes into place, the way we only have to say a few words to keep things moving, makes the afternoon fly by.

It's only when we stand back that I can see every-thing we've done. The tree house actually looks like a tree house. Even though there are two empty holes waiting for windows we can't afford yet, it's all com-ing together.

The roof and walls make it solid and real. Will looks over at me with a smile that takes up his entire face. It's a moment that doesn't need words.

CHAPTER TWENTY-TWO

The next morning, I sneak my toast and smoothie up to my bedroom to avoid the noise Josh and James are making downstairs.

Their top breakfast requests are cereal or pancakes, so Mom's green smoothie isn't going over well. I've tried teaching them the holding-your-nose-and-gulping-it-down trick and saving their toast for after, but every time, they eat all their toast and are left with an entire glass of green smoothie.

I settle into the relative quiet of my room.

Just as I finish my toast, Mom yells, "Alex! Doorbell!"

My pool bag is already packed, so I grab it and run down. But as I open the door, I realize it's not Will.

It's Rebekah.

"Hey," she says. Her shirt is tucked into her shorts just at the side, above her pocket. The rest of it falls loose. The back of her T-shirt is almost longer than her shorts. It looks good, and I kind of want to tuck mine in too, but I don't want to look like a copycat.

Josh makes a gagging sound, and James yells, "Ewwww."

Rebekah looks over my shoulder. "Is everything okay?"

"It's just my brothers." I reach for the door handle before Mom notices it's not Will, so she can't ask questions. Like why Rebekah's here or if she's going to the pool with Will and me. I'd rather feel out the answers without Mom hovering. "Bye, Mom," I call out, and close the door.

Rebekah does have a bag with her. It's straw and looks like something you'd take to the beach. "So, you headed to the pool too?" I ask.

"Yeah. My mom drives this way to work, so I asked her if she'd drop me off here. It's closer to the pool."

I nod. "You do know that Will lives . . ." I look over at Will's house.

"Oh, well yeah, but . . ." Rebekah takes her bag off her shoulder and holds it in her hands. "I actually tex-ted him last night. He said you didn't have any jobs this morning and were going to the pool. He didn't say when, though. Am I too early?"

I shake my head. "Nope, anything to leave what's going on in there." I aim my thumb at my house.

Rebekah laughs.

It's kind of nice to talk with her about everyday things. It doesn't feel like I'm scrolling through my mind, looking for something to say.

Will runs over; his hair is wet and he's got on new swim trunks. They're gray with a neon-pink stripe across the middle. I guess they're okay. Maybe it's the pink that's throwing me off.

"Cool shorts," Rebekah says.

Will's cheeks match the neon stripe. He can't even get a word out, so he just shrugs.

We stand there for a second too long, and the awkwardness creeps back in.

"So, should we go?" Rebekah asks.

Will nods and walks toward the sidewalk. Then I realize, Rebekah doesn't have a bike. I think about grabbing mine anyway, but they're already walking away. I jog to catch up.

The sidewalk is really only good for two people to walk side by side.

I trail behind them the entire way to the pool.

Rebekah pulls out a pack of watermelon bubble gum and offers Will and me a piece. I smile to myself because Will hates watermelon-flavored anything. He was eating a watermelon-flavored snow cone the day he got really sick at the school carnival in second grade. Just the smell is enough to make him gag.

"Cool, thanks." Will takes the piece, unwraps it, and chews.

"Alex, you want one?" Rebekah asks.

I'm so shocked that Will's actually chewing the gum that I shake my head.

It's just like Pops trying Greek food with Ms. Tanner. Why didn't he just tell her he prefers to eat hamburgers? Why doesn't Will just tell Rebekah "No thank you"?

By the time we finally get to the pool, Will's starving. It's only ten thirty, but his mom gives us a few slices of pizza and a tray of nachos.

Will's phone buzzes on the table. "Hey, it's Ms. Tanner."

"Don't answer it," I say too loudly.

Will holds his hands up. "Okayyy, we can call her later. I hope she's got another job for us."

I hope she's moving to Alaska and the only job she can offer us is to pack up her house into a moving van.

Will dips his slice of pizza into the nacho cheese

and leaves a trail of pizza sauce that doesn't exactly look appetizing.

Rebekah dabs her pizza with a napkin before taking a big bite. At least she finishes chewing before she asks me, "Aren't you having any, Alex?"

I grab a piece of pizza and nibble on the overflow of cheese that's gotten crunchy, but all I can think about is Ms. Tanner and Pops. I put my piece down. "I'm not really hungry."

Will grabs his third piece. "More for me."

"Are you ever afraid there won't be enough food for you?" Rebekah asks.

"That's why I eat so much. Just in case that ever happens." Will eats half the slice in a single bite. He eats the way you shove stuff into your locker between classes, and close the door just before anything can fall out. The only difference is, Will doesn't always close his mouth.

I take another bite of my pizza and hope they'll keep talking so I can stay in my head, but Rebekah turns to me again. "Hey, what was the deal with that lady the other day?"

"What lady?" Will asks. Even with pizza sauce coming out the sides of his mouth, he still manages to look surprised and a little sad. Maybe it's the fact that Rebekah knows something he doesn't.

"Ms. Tanner had a square-dance thing after our babysitting class." I hope my answer will be enough for them, because I really want to leave it at that.

"And?" Will stops eating.

"She invited Pops." I turn to Rebekah. "That's my grandpa. Anyway, Pops was there and they were, like, *together*."

Will keeps staring at me, like he's waiting for me to add more.

"Will, he was there *with* her. She's Beatrice. She's the one he's been eating Greek food with, and he brought her our family-favorite doughnuts. She's, like, his girlfriend!" Eww. I haven't said that out loud before. I don't even know if it's what you call two old people dating.

"Wait a minute." Rebekah puts her pizza down and leans closer to me. "You mean your grandpa has a girlfriend? Where's your grandma?"

"She died last year."

"Alex." Rebekah grabs my hands. "I'm so sorry. You should have told me. That's terrible. I can't believe you had to find out that way."

Her hands on my hands feels strange. I want to pull back, but at the same time, it's nice that she's agreeing with me and acts like she might just understand.

Leave it to Will to ruin the moment. "I don't think it's such a big deal."

My mouth drops open, and I stare at him. Hard.

Rebekah smacks the table. "How can you say it's no big deal?" She practically growls under her breath and turns to me. "The thing is, Alex, boys, they don't understand this stuff." She glances over her shoulder at Will and squints her eyes.

Will looks like a piece of pizza is lodged in his throat.

"You have every right to be angry about this. Your grandpa can't just replace your grandma."

I want to scream, "Thank you!" but instead I start to cry. Partly because I'm sad and partly because Rebekah's the first person to truly get how I feel. Pops is replacing Nana. Rebekah thinks so too.

"See what you did?" Rebekah whispers at Will.

"Come on, Alex." Rebekah takes my arm and leads me to the bathroom.

"What did I do?" Will asks over the noise of the pool.

The Huntington Swim Club bathroom is always dark and cool compared to outside. Rebekah pulls on the roll of toilet paper from the first stall and hands me it scrunched into a loose ball. I dab my eyes and blow my nose.

"I'm sorry," I say. Last time we were in here, I couldn't say sorry to Rebekah because I was so angry. Now I'm apologizing because I'm crying.

Rebekah shakes her head. "Don't be sorry. You have every right to be upset. I lost my dad when I was little. It's always just been my mom and me."

I look up at Rebekah, who has a small, sad smile on her face, and I feel terrible. I've been so busy hating her and judging her. Maybe her life isn't so perfect after all. She's been asking me questions and taking my side, even when Will thinks the exact opposite, and this whole time I've just been keeping my distance. *Why is she being so nice to me?*

"Listen, Alex. Once, there was this guy my mom dated when I was in fourth grade. I made up a story that he pushed me off the swing at the park when my mom wasn't looking. But I'd just fallen off. My mom freaked out. She broke up with him and wouldn't return his calls. Then one day I saw her crying in the kitchen and I knew I'd screwed it up for her." She shrugs. "You get to feel how you want about this. But, eventually, your grandpa will do whatever he wants. And, I hate to say it, but he could be really happy." She turns on the water at the sink and motions for me to come closer. She splashes some water onto my face. "It'll help take the red away. Just give it a few minutes."

I fan my face with my hands to dry the tears and water faster. How does Rebekah know about splashing water onto your face after you cry? I can't imagine her ever crying in a bathroom and trying to hide it.

Pops should be happy, but why can't our family be enough?

"Hey, girls," Samantha says, walking into the bathroom. She gets a better look at my face. "Oh no. Are you guys having a crying session?" She rushes over to the sink and holds my arms. Samantha has never been horrible to me, but she's also never been overly nice. As she gazes at me, I notice for the first time that her eyes are green.

"Sweetie, is this about Will?" she asks.

I don't even know what to say. I appreciate that she cares enough to ask why I've been crying, but Brian's dumb lovebird comment bubbles under my skin. It also seems so ridiculous. I laugh. Rebekah laughs too. And then both of us can't seem to stop laughing, and it only makes us laugh louder and harder.

Samantha lets go of my arms, opens her mouth, and squints her eyes. "What? What's so funny?"

Rebekah links her arm with mine. "Nothing. We're fine. She just stubbed her toe."

That makes us laugh more as Rebekah leads me back out into the bright sun.

Will and I stop at Mr. Edwards's on the way home. Rebekah's mom offered to drop us off, but Will quickly said no.

As we walk up the driveway, he points to Mr. Edwards's front door. "Hey, an envelope." He runs up, pulls it off the glass, and rips it open before I've caught up.

"Yes!" Will says, pulling out the cash and waving the money around. "Forty dollars!"

"Well, he did say he'd give us a bonus."

The excitement of the money seems to make him forget about being mad at Rebekah and me. He didn't say much to either of us after we came out of the bathroom.

"Another fifty or so dollars and we'll have enough for windows and some paint." Will pulls a piece of lined paper out of the envelope. It's the kind from a spiral notebook, with the jagged and frayed edges. "Hey, wait. Mr. Edwards is going away for the rest of the summer. This forty is for today's cleanup and picking up his newspapers till he's back. He took Shmoopy to his lake house." Will drops his hand to his leg, scrunching up the paper as he does. "That means this is it. This is all we have."

His head drops as he hands me the letter.

I sigh, looking over Mr. Edwards's surprisingly nice handwriting. It's not like picking up poop was the best job, but at least it was money. "I still have some flyers. We could ride around—"

"We've done that. Twice." Will snatches the bags off the porch and hands me half.

We stay close as we walk around the yard, searching for piles of poop. "I have my babysitting test soon, and then my mom will pay me."

"We could also call Ms. Tanner back," Will says softly.

"Are you serious?" I stomp over to a pile and grab it, then twist the bag around and tie a knot on top. "You really don't get it." I'm practically shaking the bag in his face. "I'm not going over there. I never want to see that lady again. I thought you finally understood."

"So what your grandpa likes her? She called again. While you and Rebekah were in the bathroom." Will shakes his head. "You're making a big deal out of nothing."

That word. "Nothing." I don't understand how a word that means "zero" and "lack of anything" can feel like something, but it does. It is heavy and sharp and digs deep, especially coming from Will, my oldest and best friend.

I pretend I'm searching for more poop, but really my eyes are blurring and there's no way I'm going to let Will see me cry. Again.

Will's phone rings.

"It's her," he says.

"No."

Will turns the phone to silent, and we don't say another word to each other even as we walk back to our houses. He doesn't stop at the end of my driveway like usual. He just goes right into his open garage, not looking back.

CHAPTER TWENTY-THREE

I'm actually glad Mom tells me that I have to babysit James and Josh on Sunday. It's a nice excuse to avoid Will. Not that I need to. He messaged to say he'd be at his grandparents' for a few days. They live on a farm, and he gets to ride four-wheelers and go fishing. Normally I get invited, but this year his grandpa is turning ninety and they're having a big family celebration.

To be honest, I'm not sure what we'd even talk about on the three-hour car ride.

As much as I don't want not being invited to bother me, it does. I'm the one who should be upset with Will, not the other way around. It sloshes around in my mind the way a drink does when you're walking and trying your hardest to not let it spill—but the more you try, the more liquid manages to go over the lip.

As I set up the backyard to entertain my brothers, I wonder if Will is relieved he doesn't have to spend the week avoiding me. Or if he's sad he can't see Rebekah.

I get the sprinkler and Dad's painting tarp out from the garage. It's not long before James and Josh are squealing and sliding all over the backyard.

I decide to grab the dish soap to make it extra fun. The family phone, which I'm waiting to be mine, buzzes on the counter as I enter the kitchen. Mom usually forgets to turn the sound back on. I grab it and answer even though I don't recognize the number.

"Hello?" I ask, digging under the sink for the big dish-soap bottle Mom uses to refill the one on the counter.

"Alex!" The voice on the other end sounds familiar, and I immediately start thinking of girls from cross-country. Maybe it's Janice? Or Tanya? "It's me. Rebekah."

"Oh. Rebekah. Hi."

"Are you busy?" she asks.

"I'm babysitting my brothers."

"Do you want to study for the CPR test together?"

"Yeah. Sure. When?"

"Is now okay?"

Rebekah was so nice at the pool the other day,

I forgot she was the girl who had wormed her way between Will and me. We connected. But things between us weren't exactly at a place where I recognized her voice or expected to get calls from her. I look down at my pajamas and touch my messy hair.

"Sure. If you don't mind helping me watch them."

"Thanks, Alex! My mom can drop me off now."

It's almost like she's eager to come over.

I'm not exactly dreading it either.

Brian is eating cereal out of a coffee mug, so I ask him to watch James and Josh while I run upstairs and get dressed.

I pull on a pale blue shirt that always makes my skin glow. I grab my running shorts since I'll probably get wet with the sprinkler on. My hair takes longer. I can't get my braid to look messy enough. I pull it out for the hundredth time and turn my head over and give my hair a shake.

Rebekah made it look so easy at the pool. I give it one more go, grabbing large chunks of my hair and crossing the pieces over and over. I don't have time to try again because the doorbell rings.

Rebekah is there, holding up her binder when I open the door. "Study time."

We wave at her mom as she backs out of the driveway.

"Took you long enough," Brian says. He puts his cereal mug in the sink without even rinsing it.

I do my best to ignore him as I lead Rebekah out back to where my brothers are playing.

Thankfully, Rebekah doesn't give Brian a moment of attention either. She has all the handouts filed in her binder, but she hasn't taken extra notes. I pass her my notebook so she can write down anything from mine that might be helpful.

"My eyes are burning," Josh says, running toward us with a bubble wand and flinging slimy bubble liquid everywhere.

"Oh, I got it," Rebekah says to me. "Let's go inside." Rebekah takes Josh's hand and leads him into the kitchen. I watch them at the sink as she turns on the water and gives him a wet dish towel to hold to his eyes.

They come back outside, and Josh sits next to Rebekah on the porch, calm and happy. I already set out chips, carrot sticks, and grapes. There was turkey for sandwiches, but only the ends of a loaf of bread, so we snack on chips as we review our notes.

"What do you do if the child is on the ground, not

responsive, but you didn't see what happened?" I ask.

"I know this one." Rebekah covers her paper with her hands. "Care fist. You put them on their side, making sure their back and neck are straight."

"Mm-hmm." I take another bite of carrot and look for a second question. "What if the child is choking?"

"Tell them to keep coughing and give them five smacks on the back, then five abdominal thrusts."

"See, I told you you'd get it."

"Thanks, Alex." Rebekah grabs another chip and closes the binder. "I'm so done with studying. I hope I pass this test Tuesday."

"I'm sure you will." I lean back in the chair and before I know it, I say, "Thanks for the other day. At the pool. You were a really good friend."

There. I said it. I called Rebekah a friend. And the thing is, it feels right. Rebekah doesn't act weirded out either; she smiles—a big smile, and waves her hand in the air like it was no big deal.

I walk into the VFW building on Tuesday afternoon to see a row of legless plastic bodies lining the floor of the hall where our tables and chairs normally are. Baby-size CPR dolls are on a table at the front, where Molly usually stands to teach.

Passing the CPR test will get me paid for the four full days of Mom's classes and seminars and fifteen random hours of babysitting I've done watching my brothers. Mom printed off a time sheet for me to keep track, and I've put down every minute. She still hasn't agreed on a dollar amount, but at least it'll be money that Will and I don't need to get from Ms. Tanner. Once Will realizes that, he won't be so mad anymore.

Molly claps her hands once everyone has arrived. "Grab your partner and sit next to a body."

Rebekah and I sit across from each other at the first body in the row, the plastic, legless CPR doll between us.

"His eyes are creeping me out," Rebekah says.

I also noticed how the eyes are the same color as the rest of it. Something about the whole situation gets Rebekah and me both giggling. That is, until Molly stands right next to Mr. Palmer, the CPR instructor, and reviews what we're doing today. He'll be watching as we perform CPR before we take our written exams.

Once we stop giggling, the test jitters set in. I run through the number of chest compressions and breaths, and I can't remember if it's two fingers or three when using compressions on a baby.

We've been watching or reading or discussing

this at some point during every class, but today Mr. Palmer and Molly will be grading us. Each partner takes a turn. Rebekah goes first.

I'm surprised how the chest of the doll bounces back and I can feel it click under my hands. It might be creepier than the skin-colored eyes. The mouth is too shallow to do a finger swipe, and the nose is too hard to squeeze closed when you breathe into the mouth.

"Great job," Mr. Palmer says. "You've completed the practical part of the exam. Let's move on to the written test."

The test is multiple choice, and I'm only not sure about two of the questions. I finish before Rebekah and most everyone else, so I read the questions again. Trevor collects our papers as we raise our hands to show we're finished.

We hover around our tables barely talking as the three adults grade our tests. Finally Molly says, "Yoo-hoo."

She stands in front of us. Trevor is next to her, holding the stack of exams.

"I can happily announce that you have all completed the six hours of training and testing you need to go out and be safe sitters! I don't want you to call yourselves 'babysitters.' You are qualified, trained, and certified to watch children safely." She bursts into applause. Everyone else is quiet because it feels strange to clap for ourselves.

Trevor calls out our names, and Molly shakes our hands as we collect our certificates.

Since there are only twelve of us in the class, the entire ceremony takes about ten minutes.

Then it's all over and we have watered-down lemonade and cookies that bring back memories of kindergarten. Even with the piece of paper, I can't help but wonder how I'll react in an emergency. A couple of summers ago, Brian was climbing in the creek and a rock fell on his toe, taking off his entire toenail. There was this bloody, fleshy gash, and Brian had to run back up to the house himself and get Mom. I just stood there. I'm good with minor scrapes and bumps, but having to perform CPR makes it feel hard to breathe.

Molly holds up some flyers, waving them in the air. "I have a list of places that are still looking for help for the rest of the summer. Most are local churches or organizations that need safe sitters once or twice a week. Feel free to take a flyer." She walks around the room handing them out.

"You two make a good team," Molly says, giving Rebekah a flyer.

Rebekah points to one that's twice a week at a church not far from here. "Hey, we could do that."

We. Even though I like the way it sounds, I'm hesitant. What if after one babysitting job she decides I'm not as cool as she thought? Or what if the other girls from class sign up and she ditches me for them? And a little part of me is worried Will is getting left out too.

"What do you think?" Rebekah asks. "Your mom could drop you off at my house and we could walk over together. That's thirty dollars a week just for this one job. I'm sure we'd be able to pick up a few extra too."

Spending more time with Rebekah doesn't seem like such a terrible thing, plus I could make more tree house or ice cream money and still not have to see Ms. Tanner.

"I'm in," I say with a smile. Will will understand once I show him the cash.

CHAPTER TWENTY-FOUR

om lets me choose what's for dinner since I passed my exam. We stop at the store to pick up stuff for burgers and grab ice cream and root beer for dessert.

"Congratulatory burgers are the best kind," Dad says as he seasons the patties. Mom fluffs the couch cushions and lights the candles in the living room that she usually saves for when we have company coming over.

Even Josh and James are in clean T-shirts, so it actually feels like graduating from my babysitting class is a real celebration.

The doorbell rings as Dad and I are about to go out back to start grilling. Our kitchen opens right into the living room, so I see her as she walks into our house.

Pops comes in behind her, holding his arm out like

she's a queen. She reaches for Josh's cheeks and ruffles James's hair. She laughs with her mouth closed, and she touches Pops's arm way too many times.

Ms. Tanner.

Beatrice.

Pops is too old to have a girlfriend.

Especially a girlfriend like Ms. Tanner.

Double-especially someone who's not Nana.

I haven't moved from the kitchen. I'm still holding the spatula and clean platter for the cooked meat.

Ms. Tanner sees me. She nods and says, "Alex."

Thankfully, she doesn't try to ruffle my hair or say I look like such a grown-up, like she said to my younger brothers. Maybe it's the way I'm standing—arms full, with my teeth pressed together so hard, even if I tried to push my spit through, I bet I wouldn't be able to.

Instead we stand there for an awkward moment before Pops claps his hands. "I sure would love a glass of tea."

Suddenly everyone's thirsty and tea is the most interesting topic of conversation.

"Let's go outside," Mom says. "Alex and Charles were just headed out to start the burgers."

I push out the door before everyone follows. Mom has already put out snacks and a pitcher of sun tea.

After saying hello to Pops and Ms. Tanner, Brian ignores everyone and stares at his phone. James grabs the entire bowl of chips and devours them from his lap. Josh doodles on some paper as Ms. Tanner goes on and on about her daughter being pregnant and how she can't wait to be a grandma.

"I've got it under control here, Al. Go grab a glass of tea." Dad nods toward the table. Then he adds, "Try for Pops."

I sit next to Pops, on the opposite side of Ms. Tanner. Josh hands her his drawing, which is just a bunch of crayon scribbles.

She overreacts and gives him a hug. It's all really gross, and I'm about to stand back up when Pops leans over and points at the tree. "I see you're almost finished with that tree house of yours."

I nod. I want to be angry at him for bringing Ms. Tanner over here without even a warning, but Pops cradles my hands in his, and it makes me feel like I'm three again, safe and loved, and the anger melts away.

"Will and I still need more money to buy the rest of the materials."

Pops smiles, his arm hanging over the back of the chair, the exact same way I sit. "I know a person who needs some work done." He nods his chin toward Ms. Tanner.

I feel like I've swallowed a gulp of lemonade the wrong way. My throat burns and my chest feels tight.

Ms. Tanner turns to Pops. "Just look what Joshie drew." Then she leans into that space where Pops's arm is hooked over the back of the chair. She fits herself right in like she's forcing Pops to put his arm around her.

I stand up, grab the pitcher, and pour some tea into a glass. "Beatrice." I say her name for the first time. Not adding a "Miss" or "Ms." Not caring if I'm being rude. "This is my nana's famous sun tea. We still use her pitcher every time we make it." I hold the glass out for her. Daring her to say no.

"Why thank you, Alex."

I know I told her to call me Alex when we met, but hearing my name come out of her mouth as she's sitting next to Pops sounds too personal, like she's a friend or a part of our family.

"My family calls me Alex. You can call me Alexandria."

Beatrice takes the cup and nods. Mom gives me a look that I can't see but can feel.

I ignore it.

In fact, I ignore all of them sitting on the porch, pretending it's okay to have this lady filling up Nana's place. I decide I no longer want to be around my family and climb up Dad's ladder that Will and I left at the bottom of the tree house. So much for a celebration. I sit in our tree house, hidden behind the walls. I know I'm acting like Josh, throwing a tantrum. I've never been so rude to an adult before. Then again, I've never had a reason to. It's not like I'm proud of acting like a brat, but I'm not exactly sorry, either.

I pull the family phone out of my pocket and call Will. I'm pretty sure he's back. The phone rings until it doesn't. Then, because I've been doing things I never thought I'd do at the start of this summer, I call Rebekah. It doesn't even ring; it just goes to a message saying the voice message system isn't set up.

I hold the phone in my hands and look out over the yard.

This whole summer I've felt like I don't fit, with Will, my family. Like one of Josh's blocks that looks like it should snap in with the rest of the set but doesn't no matter where or how hard you push it. Now, looking at the blank phone screen—no messages, no calls, no one answering, I'm not just feeling like I don't belong but that I am all alone too.

At least when you're in the way, everyone's aware of you—even if it's only because they wish you weren't there. But when you're alone, no one notices you at all.

Dad carries the burgers to the table, and Mom stands at the bottom of the tree. "Alex, wash your hands. It's time to eat." She doesn't say "please." She doesn't even wait for me to come up with a reason why I'm not hungry and don't want to join them. She just walks right back to the deck and sits next to Beatrice.

Dad gives me a sympathetic smile. "Hey, kiddo."

I avoid looking at anyone as I head inside, wash my hands, then plop down in my seat.

Pops passes me the mustard after adding a big squirt to his baked beans and another on top of his burger. He holds the bottle for a second too long and gives me a half smile. Maybe he's sad I wasn't nice to Beatrice. Maybe he wants me to apologize. Maybe he's upset with himself that he brought her here to ruin my dinner. I don't really know, and I don't want to ask.

Everyone at the table finds things to talk about all through the meal. I eat my burger slowly and am actually glad that Josh keeps needing refills of tea and more squirts of ketchup. It keeps me busy and gives me an excuse to not join in the conversation.

Michael, Will's little brother, runs over from next door as we get the fire pit going.

"Hey, bud," Dad says. "Should I grab extra marshmallows for you and Will?"

"Will won't be here till later," Michael says. "He's at the movies with his gurrrl-friend."

James does a silly dance, and Michael laughs before they chase each other around the tree.

"No running near the fire," Dad says. He puts his arm around my shoulder. "'Girlfriend'? You two know you can't have girlfriends and boyfriends until you're thirty, right?"

I roll my eyes and blink back what I really, really don't want to be tears.

Dad gives my ponytail a gentle tug before he heads up to the house.

Rebekah isn't Will's girlfriend.

But knowing that doesn't make me feel any less jealous.

CHAPTER TWENTY-FIVE

I let Wednesday go by without calling Will. It's like a fight between us that only I know is happening. So I'm probably the only one waiting for the phone to ring.

I do get a few messages. From Rebekah. She reminds me about our babysitting job that starts tomorrow. She calls twice, but I message her back, saying I'm busy and I'll see her in the morning.

I can't decide who to be mad at, Will or Rebekah. And is being jealous the same as being mad? Because they feel like the same thing.

I can't avoid Will and Rebekah forever.

On Thursday morning Mom comes up to Rebekah's door with me.

"We're just walking over to the church. You don't have to walk me to her stoop, Mom."

"It's polite." Mom pulls at the shoulder of my T-shirt to straighten it and pushes loose hair behind my ear.

Rebekah's door opens. Before Rebekah can say anything, Mom puts her hand out. "I'm so happy to finally meet you. I'm Alexandria's mom, Juliet."

Rebekah smiles and shakes Mom's hand but doesn't say anything.

"Is your mom home?" Mom asks.

Rebekah shakes her head. "No, she's at work. It's okay. I've got my own key and she'll be home by five."

Mom nods. "Okay, well, should I drop you girls off at the church?"

"Mom, it's just a street over. And there's a traffic light. With a crosswalk."

"Oh. Right. Well, I'll see you later." Mom heads to the van but doesn't drive away until Rebekah has locked the door and we're on our way down the street. She honks the horn and waves as she drives off.

"Can I tell you something?" Rebekah stops in the middle of the sidewalk and grabs both my hands.

I almost take a step back. Will never asks my permission to tell me anything. He just blurts it out. And he never grabs my hands unless it's to snatch food from me.

It's not exactly comfortable having Rebekah squeezing my hands. I kind of get a similar feeling to when Rebekah put her hand over mine at the pool. I feel trapped, but also like I'm about to share in something and I don't want her to let go.

"Okay, so don't tell anyone, but I kissed Will." Rebekah squeezes my hands with a little extra pressure and clamps her lips closed, watching my face.

I feel like there's too much spit in my mouth even though my throat burns. I flush with anger or jealousy or pain.

"Will kissed you?" I ask.

"No! *I* kissed Will."

I swear there's lava bubbling right under my skin. Flashes of heat run up and down my face and chest. Her hands are still squeezing mine. Rebekah's watching my face. I'm sure she wants me to squeal or ask her what it was like, but I'm confused.

"Why didn't you wait for him to kiss you? Aren't you supposed to . . . I don't know, let the boy kiss you first?" With each word I say, I feel more uncertain. Uncertain about kissing. Uncertain about how I feel. Uncertain about everything.

"Oh, Alex. If I waited for Will, he'd never kiss me. He's not like that." She drops my hands but scoops her arm through mine so we're walking now linked at the elbow.

I can't help but picture Will getting kissed by Rebekah. He must have turned almost purple from embarrassment the way he does whenever his mom talks about how we used to sleep in the same bed as little kids during sleepovers.

"And why should I wait for a boy to kiss me, anyway?" Rebekah asks. "I mean, he was sitting next to me in the movie theater and he whispered into my ear and there was just this moment. You know, those times when it's like you think you know what the other person is thinking, but you're not sure and if you think too much about it, you'll miss it?" Rebekah sighs. "It was like that."

Not only do I not know this feeling, but I tried my best to ignore what Michael said the other night about Will being out with his girlfriend. I mean really, how often do *my* brothers get anything right? But Michael did. "You guys went to a movie together?" I ask.

"That's not the point," Rebekah says. "The point is, we kissed."

I nod, but it doesn't matter because Rebekah's looking up at the sky and practically skipping down the sidewalk.

Would I be squealing and happy if it were any other girl with any other boy? Or if that boy and that girl weren't the ones I called, hoping they'd help me when I needed them. Instead they were together. Without me. Watching a movie. Having fun. Maybe laughing. Maybe glad I wasn't there, since neither of them invited me. And, according to Rebekah, kissing.

Rebekah stops again. The church is just ahead of us. "You're not mad, are you?"

I open my mouth, but nothing comes out. Am I?

"Oh, Alex. Please say something."

"I'm not mad." Even as I say it, that rush of emotion I can't quite place fills my chest, pulsing against my ribs so hard, words fly out of my mouth. "Will's not as innocent as you think."

I breathe in through my nose. I'm about to say something untrue, but it's the first thing I think of to release the pain that has been building up inside me. "He probably kissed some girl up in Wisconsin a few days ago when he visited his family. He's like that. He probably just never kissed you because he doesn't like you that way."

Then my feet take over and walk me away from Rebekah, away from this horrible moment, fast toward the church.

. . .

I'm in one of those moods where I just want to be sad. I could paint, I could read, I could ask Dad to come with me on a run, I could play Uno with James and Josh since they've been begging me since dinner to play a game with them, but really, I want to be in the attic. Alone.

But if Mom sees me sulking in my room, she'll force me downstairs to sit around everyone until I finally join something.

"Happiness is a pursuit, not a magnet" is exactly what she'll say. "It has to be found; it doesn't go around sticking itself to people."

So I have a book open on my chest and my water-colors on the floor next to me, just in case she peeks her head in and I need to pretend I'm doing something.

There's a knock at my door, and I wait for it to open. It doesn't. There's another knock.

"Come in," I say, holding the book so it looks like I'm reading.

Pops stands in the doorway. "Hey, you. Your dad said I could find you up here."

I push up onto my elbows and put the book at the end of my bed. "Pops. I didn't know you were here."

He shrugs. "I was really wanting a root-beer float. You up for a drive?"

I nod, and my bad mood slips away almost immediately, only a hint of it clinging to the back of my mind, where I wonder if Pops had dinner with Beatrice. But thinking about a root-beer float, just me and him, is enough to push that thought down too.

Pops leaves the windows down as we drive through town. There's something about riding with Pops in his rumbly truck that feels better in silence. Just the night air, blowing through our hair.

The best place to get a root-beer float is twenty minutes away. That may sound like a far drive for a root-beer float, but Pops and I are serious about our floats. The best floats have homemade vanilla ice cream, and the only place that does that is Aunt Lou's Frozen Treats. Pops finds the best places in the state from all the jobs he's done.

We pull into the parking lot, and Pops pushes a button on the menu. You keep your windows rolled up just a few inches, and they hook your order on a tray right on your window. They used to roller-skate up to you with trays piled high with food and ice cream. Now they just walk your tray out, but there's still something magical about eating at a drive-in restaurant.

"The usual?" Pops asks. I nod.

Our usual is two large root-beer floats and an extra-large order of curly fries with mustard.

Old-timey music plays from the outside speakers as we wait for our order.

Aunt Lou herself comes out, carrying our tray. "Thought you two forgot all about me." She hooks the tray on the window and leans her arm against the side mirror of Pops's truck door. "Alex, you are a spitting image of your gran. What grade you goin' in?"

"Eighth," I say.

She shakes her head. "Well, you two enjoy these floats. I put in extra packets of mustard. Don't be strangers, now."

She and Pops talk for a few more minutes before we're sitting quietly again. The ice cream has a nice frosted coating to it that I'm scraping off with the tip of my plastic spoon, when Pops says, "Nana loved coming here."

I twirl my spoon in my ice cream but can't quite put it into my mouth. The image of Nana enjoying a root-beer float, right here in this very seat, surfaces in my mind.

I think maybe that's all he's going to say, but then he starts again.

"Your nana was special. She is special. Never thought I'd get over losing her." He wipes his mouth with a napkin and turns to me. "I'll never really get over it, Alex, but I do like spending time with Bee. She and I both lost people we love." He waits for me to look at him. "I still love your nana. Spending time with Bee isn't going to make me forget or love Nana any less."

I nod and stare back into my float. "I know, Pops," I mumble. And somewhere deep down, I always have. Some things are easy to understand, even if they don't make any sense. Like how I know little kernels of corn will come out of the microwave as fluffy popcorn. I know it, but when I think about it too much, I can't quite figure out how it's possible. Or how someone figured that out.

Pops grabs the last three fries, drags them through the mustard, and dangles them into his mouth before washing them down with a slurp of his float.

I could let it all end there, but I need to say one more thing. I owe him that. "I'm sorry, Pops." It doesn't come out easily. The words are quiet and my voice is scratchy.

Pops nods. "I know it, Allie." He pats my knee. "Thank you."

CHAPTER TWENTY-SIX

It's only been a week since I last saw Will, but a lot has happened. For both of us. I haven't told him about my talk with Pops last night or how Pops had brought Ms. Tanner over to crash my celebratory dinner or that I've been hanging out with Rebekah. He hasn't told me about Rebekah kissing him.

If he knows that Rebekah and I have been doing things without him, he doesn't say. Just like I'm not going to bring up the movie or the kiss. Maybe I want to pretend nothing has changed, or maybe finishing the tree house feels bigger than all of that.

The sun bakes the mud, sending up the fresh smell of earth and warm grass. It's just Dad, Will, me, and the tree house.

We came out early to get most of the work done before the afternoon heat.

Dad is up on the roof, installing the skylight. Right

where Will and I can lie down and see straight up into the sky. I imagine us staring out of it, side by side.

Will and I tie off the last of the knots for our rope ladder, and Dad attaches it to the floor.

"There we have it!" Dad says, taking a break to wipe the sweat off his face. "We'll just leave the window holes open till you two can buy some."

The tree house actually looks like a tree house. It's square. The roof is slanted in just a way so that it misses the branches that arch over it. The tire swing hangs below. There's no breeze in this heat, just the buzz of a few insects, so the tire swing doesn't move or rock. It looks almost exactly like I pictured it.

Only the window holes bother me.

I thought finishing the tree house would be the glue that brought everything together. Fixing the pieces that had chipped off since summer started. Instead it looks unfinished, incomplete. Like only parts of what broke have been fixed, leaving gaps where things haven't quite worked out.

Words like "friend" and "best" used to go together like melted cheese and sauce on pizza—messy and wonderful and impossible to separate without leaving pieces of one stuck to the other. Now instead of sticking together or complementing each other, I'm left with dry bites that I don't know if I can swallow.

"I'm really proud of you two." Dad's shirt is wet at the armpits, and there's a sweat stain on his chest. Having Dad sweat so much helping us build our tree house makes it feel like a big-deal project and not just a kids' play place. Like maybe it's okay for me to think the tree house means something more.

"I'll take these hammers back to the garage, and I've gotta go check on the Sullivans' basement. You two pick up any scraps of wood and nails from the grass." Dad walks over to the garage, and Will and I are alone for the first time in almost a week.

Josh and James are at basketball camp, so no one's running through the yard breaking up the silence that wedges itself right between us. It's not just uncomfortable; it makes me sad.

I have a few nails and a large scrap of wood in my hand. "Will." I turn to face him. "You're my best friend."

I want to add: *I don't want that to change.* But when I look at him, I notice how his hair is longer and parted down the side. There's gel holding the pieces of hair at the back that usually stick up. The swoop might actually be growing on me. His T-shirt doesn't have a picture of the galaxy or a funny saying. Instead it has a brand name neatly printed exactly where a pocket would be.

Even if I don't want things to change, I realize, just by looking at Will, that things have.

Will bends down to pick up a nail.

He stands up and looks at me. His eyes are big and the darkest brown I've ever seen. They might just be the only part of him that hasn't changed. "We'll always be friends, Alex."

I nod. "Always."

Repeating the word won't make it true, but as I say it, Will nods back at me, and it feels like a pact.

It makes all the difference.

CHAPTER TWENTY-SEVEN

Rebekah doesn't call me on Tuesday morning, but she leaves me a text message about babysitting at the church.

I have an appointment. I'll meet you there.

She could be telling the truth. She could also be avoiding having to spend any extra time walking there with me. I guess I don't blame her. I was pretty awful to her the last time we spoke.

I have to say, I don't like the way it feels to be on this side of things. I was the one trying to avoid her for so long. Now that she's trying to stay away from me, I can't ignore how mean I've been—even if it was her fault to begin with. Still, I've actually liked hanging out with her. I've liked being able to share things with someone who's not Will.

Mom pulls up to the church. "You're sure Rebekah didn't need a ride?"

"No, we're meeting here." I grab for the door. James and Josh throw a ball back and forth, and James kicks my seat forward, again. At least the kids we watch sit and color and like playing Ring around the Rosie.

Mom reaches for my arm. "Alex, you sure everything's okay?"

"Mo-oom." I push open the door, but when I catch a glimpse of her, she looks how I've been feeling most of summer: confused and sad. I lean back into the car. "Mom, really. I'm okay." I lean in and kiss her on the cheek.

Mom smiles. "Have a great day," she says.

I close the door and jog toward the church.

Mrs. Williams, the woman in charge of the babysitters, is waiting in the hallway. She gives me my lanyard with my name. I loop the name tag over my head and take the storage tub with our classroom number on it.

No one's in the room yet, so I put up the instruction signs with sticky tack so parents know where to put their children's bags and where to sign them in. Then I set out the coloring supplies on one table and wooden puzzles on another.

Rebekah runs in just as I'm pulling out a few books.

"Hey," she says quietly.

"Hey," I reply. "How was your appointment?"

"My appointment?" Rebekah looks confused, but recovers quickly. "Oh, yeah. My appointment. It was good."

She busies herself with the sign-in clipboard, name-tag stickers, and pens for the parents' table.

Even as the kids start to arrive, Rebekah and I stay in our halves of the room. We don't talk; we don't get close enough to bump elbows or give each other a look when one of the kids does something silly. I know I should say I'm sorry. I do feel half responsible, but the other half is her doing. It's like when you play a game. Do you say sorry when you win? It's not the winner's fault for winning, if that's the whole point of playing the game. I'm not saying Will is some kind of prize that Rebekah and I are competing for. But I also wouldn't have had to make up the part about Will kissing lots of girls if she hadn't gone and forced a kiss on him.

Every time I think of that kiss, I'm not sure if the burning under my skin is me wishing I'd been there to save Will, or if I secretly want a first kiss of my own.

Rebekah reads a book to a small group of kids, and I'm sitting at the coloring table, watching her, thinking about how much has happened in the last few weeks, when Thomas starts gagging. I stand up, but can't move beyond that. His face gets red, and all the things I should be doing run through my head. Pat his back, do a mouth-swipe, say "Keep coughing." It's all right there but I'm frozen in place.

Rebekah pushes past me. She hits Thomas on the back five times. "Keep coughing, Thomas. Keep coughing." Rebekah's voice is calm and sure. She looks at me. "I can see it. There's a crayon piece in his mouth." She turns back to Thomas. "I'm going to hit your back again, Thomas. Keep coughing." She hits his back five more times, and Thomas coughs out the piece of crayon. It's green and wet, and it lands right on the table with a mixture of a splat and a thud.

Rebekah falls into a chair and holds Thomas in her lap. He bursts into tears, and the room goes from the sound of Thomas coughing to the sound of every child crying. I look around and don't know who to help first.

Again my feet and brain short-circuit. Rebekah doesn't wait for me. "Get a cup of warm water and find Mrs. Williams. Hurry." She holds Thomas, stands up, and starts singing and marching around the room. The kids stop wailing; the tears are still falling down their faces, but they follow her. I finally snap out of it and grab a cup from the snack tray. I head down the hall, looking in each door for Mrs. Williams as I make my way to the bathroom.

She's in a classroom with rocking chairs and babies.

"Mrs. Williams, we need you down in the five- and six-year-old room." She jogs out the door, and I point toward our classroom. "I just have to get some warm water."

When I make it back to the classroom, Rebekah is marching around the classroom, singing "If You're Happy and You Know It." Mrs. Williams is sitting with Thomas. I hand her the cup of water.

"There, there. Take little sips." She nods at me and waves her hand for me to join Rebekah. We march one more circle, still singing, and then I pull out a book and start reading, giving Rebekah a break. We play a few games and have a snack that nobody really touches, before the parents come for pickup.

Mrs. Williams meets Thomas's mom at the door and explains what happened. Thomas hugs Rebekah. "She got me to cough the green crayon onto the table."

I'm afraid we'll get in trouble, but Thomas's mom hugs Rebekah too. "Thank you. He's always putting things into his mouth at home. I should have warned you." Thomas waves and blows kisses as they go down the hall.

Mrs. Williams turns to us. "You two did exactly what you were supposed to. Wonderful job."

Rebekah doesn't tell her how I was no help at all. How she did it herself.

We clean up the room, still avoiding each other, but now that it's quiet, especially after Thomas's choking, it's harder and harder to leave my sorry unsaid.

I throw away the wipes I used to clean the tables and stand close to where Rebekah is putting the signs and name tags in a container that we store in the classroom tub. "I'm really sorry. About today, about—"

"You know what?" Rebekah says, not taking a breath for me to answer. "I've tried really, really hard. I've been nice to you. And all you've done is be mean." She clicks the lid of the container in place and steps toward me. "If it hadn't been for me, who knows what would have happened to Thomas." She lets that sink in as she shoves the container away. She slams the cabinet door, grabs her bag, and turns back around. "It's not my fault if Will likes me more than you." She stares at me. Maybe she's waiting for me to respond. Maybe she has more to say.

All I can do is squirm. My toes feel stiff and uncomfortable in my sandals. My throat is dry and scratchy. My hands feel like an extra part of my body that doesn't fit anywhere.

Rebekah rolls her eyes, then walks out the door. I can hear her shoes slap down the tile hallway. The church organ starts playing a sad, drawn-out song, and I race after Rebekah.

"Wait," I call out as I run to catch up with her. She's almost at the main door.

"You're right. I don't know what happened to me today. I really am sorry. And I'm sorry about what I said about Will not liking you. I'm sorry I didn't know how to treat you this whole summer. It's just—"

All those gaps between my "I'm sorry"s. The excuses for why I did what I did don't really matter now. Because, when I think about it, Rebekah is just reacting to how I've been treating her. She probably didn't want me to join her and Will at the movies or to swim in the pool because every time it's been the three of us, I haven't exactly been the friendliest person.

"Rebekah, it's always been Will and me. I've never had many other friends, let alone girls who are friends, and I wasn't sure how to react. I was worried you were taking him away. But you were nice to me, in class and inviting me to your house, and helping me study for the CPR test. And you're the only one who understood about my Pops." I take a deep breath. I didn't realize just how good a friend Rebekah has been until I said it all out loud. "I'm sorry I haven't done the same."

Rebekah stands at the big church door. Her hands are on the push bar, but she doesn't open it. She doesn't look at me either.

Finally she drops her arms and turns to me. "Alex, I'm sorry about Will. I didn't mean to start, you know, *liking* him. I was trying to say hi to you both that day at the pool, but Will was the only one who said hi back. You guys seemed to be having so much fun, and I just wanted to hang out with you. To be honest, I was kind of scared of you the first time we met. I didn't mean for it to get so complicated. Don't get me wrong, Will is cute and funny—"

Shoes click toward us and a lady clears her throat. "Excuse me, girls."

Rebekah and I turn to see an older lady wearing a dark-colored dress peer at us over her glasses.

"This is the house of God. Can you please discuss boy matters outside?"

I can feel the heat spreading across my cheeks. Rebekah's eyes go wide. She grabs my arm and pulls me through the big church doors. Once they slam behind us, Rebekah cracks up. "The house of God?" she says, laughing.

I laugh harder. There's a knock on the tall, thin window behind us. The lady narrows her eyes in our direction. Giggles pour out of us, and Rebekah runs down the stairs, waving me after her. I can barely keep up, I'm laughing so hard. We don't slow down until we're around the corner.

"I feel bad," I say when I've finally caught my breath.

"Why?" Rebekah asks between laughs.

"I don't know." I take a few more deep breaths and look at Rebekah. Her ponytail droops, and stray hairs stick to her forehead. Something about her standing outside, crusty glue on her T-shirt and jean shorts that look exactly like a pair I have, makes the things wedged between us this summer—like green bikinis, Will, worrying if she's nice or just using me to find out more about my best friend—all melt away, taking with it the sadness and anger and jealousy I was holding on to.

Right now it's just me and a girl who's fun to hang out with. A girl who might just be my new friend.

CHAPTER TWENTY-EIGHT

The rain comes down hard; the branches of the tree just outside the den window tap against it, almost in sync with Josh's kicks. He bangs his heels into the floor and flails on the ground, all while using his baby voice to say "no-no-no" over and over again. He's done it since he was little, sitting in his high chair. He's always said "no" in threes. I used to think he thought it was a single word.

Now he's old enough to know he's just being a big baby. James picked up his half of the game pieces and is now happily on the couch with the tablet.

"You can choose the show after lunch," I say. I'm all out of ideas with him. Mom's been on calls since early this morning, and Josh woke up in a bad mood. He still hasn't brushed his teeth, and he's wearing his pajama shorts and nothing else.

"Look, I can't get lunch ready if you don't behave."

I'm not expecting it to work, but Josh stops rocking back and forth. He stops saying no. He does keep hitting his heels hard against the floor. "I'll let you spread the butter," I say, giving in and using a singsong voice.

Finally he sits up and puts his arms zombie-like in front of him. He shuffles behind me to the kitchen. "We have to wash our hands first." I reach to help him up onto the footstool near the sink, but he pulls away from me, falling back and hitting his elbow hard against the cabinet handle and then the floor.

He bursts out into a loud wail and kicks at me when I bend down to help him. "Go away!" he shouts, striking his feet in my direction.

"Josh, please stop," I say, putting my hands in front of me to protect myself from his kicks.

"Did you push him?" James asks, walking into the kitchen with the tablet.

"Of course not. Get his blankie so he'll calm down."

James walks back into the den to get Josh's blanket, and I sit down next to him, waiting for him to stop crying.

"Yoo-hoo!" a voice calls from the front door.

I have no idea who it can be, and Mom's still in her office, so I get up, leaving Josh, and rush to the door. Ms. Tanner is standing there, her umbrella barely keeping her dry.

I should say "Come in," or "Hello" at the very least, but I haven't seen her since the last time she came over for my celebratory dinner, and I only apologized to Pops for that night. I'm thinking all this and wondering if I should start off with an apology, when she steps inside, quickly closing the door behind her. Her umbrella drips on the rug in the entry. "I don't mean to bother you. I tried calling your mom."

"She's working," I say. Josh lets out a loud wail. For attention.

"Oh no, is this a bad time?" she asks.

I shake my head and Josh gets louder. "Sorry, I just have to check on Josh."

"Let me help." Ms. Tanner drops her umbrella in the holder next to the pile of our shoes and slips out of her sandals. She's holding a box that's wrapped like a present and a clear plastic container of cookies that have a store sticker; I don't offer to take either.

Josh is still on the floor, holding his blanket, but crying with his mouth and no tears.

"What happened, Joshie?" Ms. Tanner asks. She puts what's she's holding on the counter before bending down closer to Josh.

He loves being treated like a baby when he's in this kind of mood, so when Mrs. Tanner calls him "Joshie," he stops crying and sticks out his bottom lip.

"I'm hungry," he says.

"Well, it looks like Alexandria is trying to make you lunch." She holds her arms out to him. Josh sits up and falls into them.

I don't know why it hurts just a little, hearing her call me Alexandria. I know I told her to, but hearing her say it and call Josh "Joshie" is like being called someone's second-best friend. Even when you know it's true and you feel the same way about that person, there's still a sting attached.

"Do you want to show Ms. Tanner the fairy puzzle?" I ask.

"Who's Ms. Tanner?" Josh asks.

"Me, Beatrice." She looks up at me after she tells Josh.

I nod. "Sorry. Beatrice." Her name comes out more easily than I expect.

Josh leads her into the den, and I can hear him jabbering on and on about the fairy cartoon he loves, telling her each of the fairies' names.

I get started on the grilled cheese and make an extra. Maybe in case Beatrice stays or maybe in case

James wants another. Mom already has carrot and celery sticks washed and cut in the fridge, so I grab some of each and put them on a plate with a small bowl of ranch dressing. I let the grilled cheeses sit for a few minutes so the cheese won't gush out all over the plates when I cut them.

Beatrice laughs and asks Josh lots of questions. I even hear James laugh a few times. I don't want to listen in, because even though Pops said no one will replace Nana, it's hard to believe that when Nana isn't here. When she isn't the one playing with my brothers, making them laugh.

At least the cookies Beatrice brought are store-bought. Nana only ever came over with homemade cookies. But these cookies are from the organic place Mom likes, and they're salted caramel, which isn't something Nana would have ever tried to make. She stuck to what she knew: chocolate chip. And on more special occasions: apple pie. Snickerdoodles at Christmas and vanilla cake with vanilla buttercream frosting for birthday cupcakes.

I put the cookies where James and Josh can see them, but they know they have to eat their carrots and celery first.

"Lunch is ready," I say.

James and Josh come running into the kitchen, and this time Josh doesn't throw a fit about washing his hands.

Beatrice follows, and I offer her the extra grilled cheese.

"Why, thank you."

I drag my piece through mustard, and Beatrice smiles at me. "My Howard loved mustard on his grilled cheese too."

Ms. Tanner saying her dead husband's name makes me sad. I look up from my plate. I'd forgotten she was the nice lady who gave Will and me a job and lots of cookies, and not just a stranger getting close to Pops. I'd done it more than once this summer.

"Pops likes mustard too," I say.

Beatrice smiles. "I noticed." We're quiet for a moment before she pats my hand and says, "Thank you."

I quickly move my hand out from under hers and push the plate of vegetables toward my brothers. "You have to have three of each before you get a cookie."

The boys grab the carrots and celery sticks and cover each bite in ranch dressing before eating them.

"You know, Alexandria," Beatrice says, "I've been trying to get ahold of you and Will. Are you two still looking for jobs?"

I'm glad I have a bite of grilled cheese in my mouth so I can shrug and not have to tell her the truth: that I've been avoiding her.

"I wanted to paint my front door to match the garage door. And now that my daughter gave birth, I'm going away for a few weeks to visit her. I thought you and Will could water my plants for me."

"Plants?" I ask. "I thought they were all fake."

"Yes. They were. But I went to the nursery the other day." She chews her food slowly. Like maybe she's trying to figure out how to say what she means. She puts her sandwich down and looks at me. Her eyes hold mine. "Buying real flowers is my way of turning over a new leaf, so to speak."

I know from Mom that adults often say one thing and mean another. I think Beatrice means that Howard has been gone a long time and she's ready for something new. That might just be hanging out with Pops and buying real flowers instead of keeping fake ones.

It's hard to say how that makes me feel. Thankfully, Mom walks out of her office and she and Beatrice take a few minutes to catch up on what's been going on. I open the cookies for the boys and put the plates in the sink and try to slip away, but Beatrice reaches for my arm.

"Alexandria," she says, her voice soft. I consider telling her to call me Alex instead, but I'm still thinking about it.

She grabs the present off the counter and hands it to me. "This is for you."

I hold it out in front of me. It's really, really heavy. I can't imagine what could possibly be in there. "Thanks," I say quietly.

Beatrice is still looking at me. The same way she did when she told me about her plants. I wonder if she wants me to open it. I hate opening gifts in front of people. Even if I like the gift, I end up acting like I don't because everyone's staring and I feel weird.

I reach to pull off the wrapping paper, but Beatrice puts her hand on mine. "Not now. Open it after I've gone."

I nod, and Mom smiles at me.

Josh reaches for another cookie, and Mom immediately asks, "How many carrots did you have?"

With everyone distracted, I sneak up to my room with Beatrice's present.

CHAPTER TWENTY-NINE

With only one full week of summer left, we now have every part of the tree house nailed in place. Well, almost every part. The windows were too expensive, but Beatrice helped with that. Will and I hung up her gift right where the window holes were: stained-glass panels made from Nana's glasses I broke. When Dad told Pops what I'd done, Beatrice heard and asked if she could make something with the broken glass.

The panels are rectangles and smaller than the window holes, but they cover most of them. They hang from a gold chain that Dad let us nail up ourselves.

Will lies next to me, one arm bent behind his head. The other is slung across his chest as he stares out the skylight.

The branches above us sway and make it feel like

we're on a ship, way out at sea. Maybe even on a deep-sea diving expedition. That day at the pool, playing our game and meeting Rebekah, feels like years ago. It's even hard to remember what the tree looked like without our tree house.

"Swimming conditioning starts Monday," Will says.

"Cross-country, too," I add.

"Nights are all we'll have up here." Will's voice is soft. Maybe sad. Maybe just tired.

"Yeah," I say quietly. I'm not ready to let go of summer.

Actually, I'm not ready to let go of a lot of things. Like long days at the pool with Will and Rebekah. Or babysitting at the church. Or biking around the neighborhood.

Other things I'd like to forget, like being horrible to Rebekah and Ms. Tan—Beatrice. Even wasting my time being mad at Will. He still hasn't said anything about the kiss with Rebekah, but even that feels pointless now. I don't need to know everything. Our friendship is bigger than that.

The sun falls the tiniest bit, barely noticeable unless you're watching. Light streams through the stained-glass window. The tree house glows a warm yellow, with a shine that's green and little pieces of blue. The jagged bits of broken glass turn the room into what I would think the middle of a Christmas tree looks like: brown and glowing yellows, reds, blues, and greens that bounce like prisms across the walls.

Beatrice's gift is the perfect addition to our tree house. Nana's broken glasses complete our summer challenge. Now she's a part of our new memories, too.

I'm sure Will would agree that this challenge is our best one.

I think about all those folds in my brain. All the moments stored away in there. Some I don't even remember at first, but they're there when I need them.

This summer is there now. Tucked away.

Maybe at the beginning, things with Will and me felt like shattered glass. But now, at the end, having Rebekah around has been more like a new and unexpected color of stained glass—exactly the right addition.

The three of us hold on to the raft way out in the deep end. Rebekah's in the middle. Will's at the end. My elbows are lopsided because I'm at the top with the pillow part.

"You don't have to be fast, right? It's more about endurance?" Rebekah keeps asking about cross-country.

"Yeah, but obviously being faster means you'll place higher and get more points for the team."

"When are you buying your shoes? Have you been practicing this summer?" she asks excitedly.

"I don't know. Next week, maybe. I only really practice when we're in season, but my parents said I have to get more serious in high school."

Rebekah sighs. She doesn't seem to have any more questions at the moment, and I can catch my breath.

"You should do swimming instead," Will says.

"No way, too early in the morning." Rebekah turns back to me. Will splashes at the water with his hands, his eyes fixed downward.

"Let me know when you're going to buy your shoes. I'll ask my mom to take me then too."

"Sure." It will be nice to practice with someone before conditioning starts.

Will keeps splashing at the water. He doesn't need to say he's feeling left out. I can tell by the way he bites at the inside of his bottom lip and flares his nostrils.

"Hey, guys," Samantha says from the side of the pool. She has a pair of shorts thrown on over her suit. "Brian'll be here soon. You need a ride home?"

Ever since Samantha saw Rebekah and me in the bathroom that day, she's been extra nice and had Brian stop teasing me that Will's my boyfriend. I always thought she didn't pay attention to me because we were so different, but I guess all along she noticed more than I did.

As much as a ride home sounds good, there's no way I'm going to shorten this day at the pool.

"We're okay. Thanks, though," I say.

Samantha waves as she leaves.

I throw a few diving sticks into the pool. It's not as loud today, so you can hear each one *splash* as it hits the surface. School doesn't start for a few more days, and I'm already missing summer.

"We should run tomorrow. How about around your neighborhood before we babysit?" Rebekah says.

"Okay," I reply. "You want to join us, Will?"

He shrugs and stops splashing the water. "Okay." Then he looks at me. "If you don't mind."

"Whoever gets the most sticks gets a ten-second head start on tomorrow's run!" I call out, already diving under the water.

ACKNOWLEDGMENTS

The idea for this book started with a memory from my childhood. So, first, I have to thank my cousin Will for all the fun times we had growing up and for inspiring the catalyst of this story.

Thank you, Patricia Nelson, for always helping me polish and refine my ideas and continuing to champion my books.

Many thanks to Liz Kossnar for being excited about this book when it was just a couple of pages long and to Krista Vitola for enthusiastically taking over, helping me get rid of all my echoes—sorry!!

The Simon & Schuster team has always taken great care in creating covers that embody my stories—and they've done it again! Thank you to everyone there who has a hand in turning my words into a book.

Mark Holtzen, you have been with this book since it started. Your snarky comments and pointy finger keep me in line. Thank you.

A few days away in Indy with Elizabeth Slamka for the Annual Good Times Smorgasbord Extravaganza was the respite I needed as I wrapped up this book. You and Devoll are the best. Speaking of human teeth, meatballs! (That's for you, Cristina Slamka.)

My family is always an inspiration, not only for characters and scenes but also in general. Mom and Dad, you have prayed for me continually since I was in fourth grade. I know that I'm where I am today with all thanks to you both. My Grandpa King passed away as I wrote this book, and a lot of him is in Pops. Thanks to Grandma Sylvia for never belittling my dream to be an author and buying me a book on how to write way back when I was in third grade. Every time I use spell check, I think of you.

Thanks to my husband for pushing my books on your colleagues and wanting the best for our family. My children might never actually read my books, but they are the first to brag about me—thank you.

And, always, thanks to my Heavenly Father.